Big Business

A FABLE

GERRY HUERTH

LitPrime Solutions
21250 Hawthorne Blvd
Suite 500, Torrance, CA 90503
www.litprime.com
Phone: 1-800-981-9893

Published by LitPrime Solutions: 10/06/2023

ISBN: 979-8-88703-291-7(sc)
ISBN: 979-8-88703-292-4 (e)

Library of Congress Control Number: 2023915359

Contents

Chapter 1

At 2 a.m. a cool breeze ruffled the humid night with a promise of relief and almost by accident brushed through an old cotton wood tree. The dreaming leaves stirred with barely a complaint and released thousands of tiny parachuted seeds to float across the summer moon. They roamed in a ghostly flurry of possibilities searching for unsuspecting yards in which to land, sprout, and grow with such irrevocable speed that they couldn't all be casually destroyed as nuisances.

On their pilgrimage of chance they swirled by a tall gaunt house with one yellow lit window on its second floor. On the other side of that window George was dying. His daughter Mary, the nurse, fumbled to inject the last shot of morphine, easing the breaths that tore through the cavern of his mouth. In a far shadowy corner of that same bedroom the younger prettier daughter, Belinda, lit a small blue feather and set it on a cracked saucer. As the feather flickered out,

George's desperate gasps softened then stopped; the look of apprehension that had filled his last breathless years passed into the unexpected breeze.

Their mother, Helen, who burnished her grief those next few months in a frenzy of house cleaning, cooking, and apprehension for her two unmarried daughters, wilted before the first frost. A heart attack grasped her hand one night leaving a limp corpse behind. In the course of that summer, the two daughters were left with the old family home newly mortgaged to pay medical and funeral costs, each other, and a sense of dread that was barely mitigated by the fact that at least now there was no one left to worry about them.

Chapter 2

$\mathcal{E}$verybody said that Mary had a nice personality. She stood tall and raw boned like her father. The firmly cleft chin belied her fluttery eyes. Her large pastel clad frame moved haltingly as if careful apprehension could at least delay disaster. Perhaps it was that chin jutting forward from her dainty stem of a neck or just the years of nursing; but something barely short of determination animated her circuitous journey through life. After all Belinda said that Mary was very brave.

Of course Belinda never left the house any more. Years ago she began confining her slim form and wild eyes to the parameter of the yard; neighbors began nodding their heads describing her as "delicate," uncertain if this were a talent or a malady.

Belinda's communication with the world was now limited to the envelopes and coupons pushed through the slot in the front door by a uniformed person at approximately 11 a.m. every day except Sunday. Those various sheets of junk mail that most people automatically brush away like gnats, served as a lifeline and deep source of interest to her.

A clear summer morning dawns on the shabby urban neighborhood. Urgent looking people with steely expressions on their faces are rushing out of their houses towards their cars. Mary Blu, dressed in her white uniform slowly trudges down the street coming home from her night shift. She heads toward the ramshackle house at the end of the street that dead ends at a run down little playground squeezed against a gray industrial park. A few cottonwood seeds float by her unnoticed.

Belinda, face wild with excitement and dressed in a frayed kimono, springs at tired Mary as she cautiously enters the dilapidated living room.

"Mary, you wouldn't believe!"

Mary looks down. "Things didn't go so well..."

Belinda is ecstatically waving a color brochure in Mary's face. "It's just wonderful Mary, amazing! There's a big meeting at the Convention Center. Everybody who's anybody will be there, and it's tonight!"

"I don't know. I tried to be more careful..."

"It's the Harmonic Convergence! Do you hear me? The Harmonic Convergence!"

Mary reluctantly studies the brochure that is pressed towards her face. "But..."

"Shamans from Siberia, a woman who channels

Nostradamus, even Milton Marsalis, you know the man who wrote that book; they're all going to be there...tonight!"

Mary stares at the fierce excitement in Belinda's face.

"You have tonight off. We need to go!"

"You always say we." Mary closes her eyes.

Belinda pouts. "You're such a ninny. You never do anything. What would you do without me?"

"But you never go out, not since..."

Belinda turns away frantically and starts humming.

Mary watches.

Belinda begs. "Please, pretty please; just this once for me?"

Mary heaves a resigned sigh.

"It'll be wonderful, you'll see." Belinda starts flapping around the room like a tattered butterfly. "You're so brave Mary; you can do it."

Chapter 3

$\mathcal{M}$ary spends most of the day anticipating her venture, trying on one outfit after another. It's not that she really cares about how she looks. Uncertainly zigzagging between her closet and bed, piles of clothes form on the pink bedspread. Not that she has any pretensions to attractiveness; she simply wants to somehow fit into a situation that is beyond the boundaries of her tightly reigned imagination. She intently studies her bed, eyes moving from pile to pile to pile and then back again. With each new circuit her eyes widen more in panicky confusion. Finally she shudders, closes her eye and slowly spins around once, twice, and three times. Eyes still tightly closed, her hand reaches out and settles on one of those piles of clothes. She opens her innocent eyes and studies the pastel green skirt with a lacy beige blouse that rests under her hand. Yes, that will do, maybe. The high collar might even camouflage that embarrassingly thin neck of hers.

Unfortunately although not altogether unexpectedly, Belinda is too busy to leave the house that evening, either writing a new poem or transplanting a begonia; she isn't sure.

But something like determination pushes Mary out of that home on the dead end street of her childhood to a rendezvous with the New Age. Mary really doesn't know what the New Age is. Of course she has seen the Wizard of Oz at least twenty times and has a little golden angel pin which she wears on special occasions. In reluctant moments of introspection she even occasionally notices some sort of shifting deep down in her core as if some very reluctant being is stirring in there. Although at those embarrassing moments she simply takes an antacid and returns to the important duties usually involving taking care of someone.

Mary walks hesitantly from the house and onto the cracked sidewalk, her feet obliviously stirring up drifts of cottonwood seeds as she looks over the brochure in disbelief. She stops and glances back uncertainly at Belinda who stands in the doorway decked out in a faded purple dress.

Belinda shoos Mary away with her hands and yells, "It'll be wonderful! Just pretend you're off to see the Wizard of Oz."

Mary swallows her fear and turns back to follow her pilgrimage into the New Age.

Slowly she walks into the summer evening, not noticing how the setting sun shines golden on the shimmering cotton wood leaves. Rubbing her stomach uneasily, she halts and peers into the jumbled contents of her large black purse; her hands search it desperately. She grasps a little piece of paper in her shaky hand; her feet empowered by some mysterious force start carrying her further up the block.

She stops at the corner just as a bus roars through the quiet evening street. It stops in front of her and spreads open its accordion doors. Her face tightening in panic; she steps up those stairs and into her future.

She glances at the bus driver. "Does this go past the Convention Center?"

He nods nonchalantly.

"I mean the Minneapolis Convention Center."

He stares at her. "Lady, we're in Minneapolis."

"I'm sorry, it's just I didn't..." her small voice disappears into apology.

His eyes turn away from her. "Just relax, take a seat. I'll let you know when it comes up." He stares at her in the windshield shaking his head he drives off, leaving Mary to stagger toward a seat.

Twenty minutes later the bus stops in front of a grand looking building. The driver's eyes stare into the rear view mirror at Mary sitting nervously in her seat. He calls out in a ringing voice. "The Minneapolis Convention Center."

She jumps up and rushes frantically toward the front.

Those eyes in the rear view mirror are examining her. "Okay lady, it's not going anywhere."

"I'm sorry. I just didn't…"

"Watch your step."

She walks down the stairs and through the opening doors, her face congeals into a frozen mask; only her eyes betray her panic.

The bus roars away as she stands motionless on the sidewalk. Bewildered, she looks up; towering above her stands a massive building. She examines it closely as people rush by her. Edging closer to a wide granite stairway she finally takes one tentative step and then another. She keeps ascending the stairs until she finds herself standing in front of a tall revolving glass door. Impatient pedestrians keep pushing through it setting those glass panels spinning faster and faster. She makes a couple of false starts, but each time balks letting the revolving doors exclude her. Finally in desperation she closes her eyes and in she steps. Surprised, she stares out of her glassed in compartment waiting for her release. Then she is deposited there, in the Minneapolis Convention Center, face to face with a large sign: "Welcome To the New Age." A large arrow points her toward a grand stairway.

Cautiously, step by step, she hazards her way up another set of stairs, this time marble. At the summit a large star-sparkled banner beckons to her. She is too embarrassed to examine it closely but notices the name "Milton Marsalis" in bold dramatic letters. She checks the name on her piece of crumbled paper and tip toes through the door into the dimly lit cavernous gloom. Crowds of shadowy people inside are already sitting in hushed anticipation of the New Age.

As inconspicuously as possible she totters down the shadowy aisle glancing from side to side trying to find a seat. Suddenly a spot light flashes on the stage. Gasps of awe rise from the audience; a flashily suited little man springs into that radiant circle.

The hall breaks out in thunderous applause.

He stares hypnotically into his congregation. Solemn silence settles over the hall. Dramatically as if in a trance he raises his arms and proclaims, "Life is sacred!"

Mary's face flushes in embarrassment as she attempts to shrink her bulk as she haltingly continues her way down the shadowy aisle, glancing from side to side searching for an empty seat. Each time she glances down a row of occupied seats, she shakes her head and moves on deeper into the heart of darkness.

The audience bellows back. "Life is sacred!"

There, she finally spots an empty seat in the middle of a crowded row. Trying desperately to look composed, she clumsily squeezes in front of the ecstatic people.

Milton calls out, "There are no accidents!"

The crowd echoes back, "There are no accidents!"

Mary stumbles in front of a bellowing woman. "Oops, I'm sorry…so sorry…didn't mean to…"

Mary stumbles into the seat. She's found an island of safety at last. Her bulky form settles into the seat.

Milton announces, "Be ready for miracles!

A something pokes her from behind.

The crowd answers, "Be ready for miracles!"

Mary's startled scream is drowned out by the crowd.

Milton, with a beatific smile on his face whispers, "The universe cares about you."

Very cautiously Mary turns around to peek at the source of the intrusion.

The crowd whispers back, "The universe cares about you."

A diminutive, crimson clad figure, coal black pixie hair, glittering intense eyes, and blood red lipstick stares at Mary with burning intensity.

Milton cries out, "Dare to be you!"

The crimson figure in a deep and demanding voice says, "Mary Blu."

Bewildered, Mary squints at that figure.

The crowd cries out, "Dare to be you!"

Pressured by the anticipation of those intense eyes, Mary smiles in shy confusion while her large head nods on that thin stalk of a neck. Mary flutters her gaze across this entreating stranger. On one of those fluttery passes a tiny explosion of recognition ignites Mary's memory--yes, Rita, Rita Reinke: the reunion begins.

Milton smiles in satisfaction. "Trust the universe."

Mary's mind, so used to trying to forget, alights

with memory. After all it had been twenty years since Rita had been in charge of the acquisition's department at the college library. There she had wrestled with the twin tasks of cataloging all new materials and making sure Mary stamped the university logo with absolute, centered precision on the first page of each new book. Back then Rita had also enhanced her diminutive height with a towering precisely chiseled red wig.

The crowd smiles and says, "Trust the universe,"

Those puzzle pieces form into a memory from her avoided past, yes, that initial meeting with Rita. As Mary handed the very first and slightly crumbled job application of her life to this small person with larger than life arms and wig, Mary found herself whirling in Rita's flood of grand plans and poignant insights. Indeed Mary found herself recognized as a very special person elected to appreciate the depths of Rita's soul.

Milton cries out, "The universe has a purpose for you!"

As the crowd answers, "The universe has a purpose for you," Rita whispers in Mary's ear, "Come with me." Rita, clutching a pink purse, plows her way out of the auditorium without looking back; she knows Mary is in tow.

Mary scrambles frantically to follow.

It is an evening in late June. Even at 9PM, reflected sunlight on glassy skyscrapers shine against the darkening sky. The pungent smells of grass newly mown that afternoon could almost make a cautious person hope. As Mary brushes off a bench for her guest, something, something rustles through her closed life, half romance, half sorrow, a flurry of feeling in her stomach that things were about to… she really doesn't have a word for it.

Rita, like a queen at a coronation sits down on her throne. She strikes a dramatic pose as she gazes at the first evening star.

She whispers, "The stars control our lives."

Mary glances up at the sky and nervously sits down next to Rita.

Rita smiles mysteriously. "This meeting was meant to be."

From inside The Convention Center the faint sound of applause mixes with the nearby street sounds.

Rita pierces Mary with her shining eyes. "When did I see you last?"

Mary starts to open her mouth.

Rita shakes her head urgently. "It doesn't matter. I live in the eternal present." A siren screeches a block away. Jolted by the piercing sound, her air of mystery disappears, and she is transformed. Her voice becomes childishly plaintive. "Daddy says I am a good girl." She starts rocking gently back and forth on the bench, singing, "Twinkle, twinkle little star. How I wonder what you are."

Mary looks away.

Rita's two large hands suddenly grab onto the seat of the bench, anchoring her against the disturbance of the siren. As the screeching sound disappears in the distance, her body is transformed once again taking on a heroic posture. She looks off into the distance with fierce determination. "I help people now. Goddamn assholes always get in my way!"

Mary looks at Rita sideways and opens her mouth as if she is going to say something.

Rita charges ahead, "After you left, I had that run in with the administration. They treated me horribly, but I showed them, you bet your bad ass I did. I left them in the dust and moved on to a new library in the city that was just begging for my vision. Within a year, that place hummed like a finely tuned machine. You know how I like everything to be just right."

Mary nods remembering that file drawer at the university library labeled "Broken Pencils, Too Small to Use."

Rita rushes forward. "It was then I met Hans. My life blossomed. I even threw out that wig; Hans said my own black hair made me look dangerously sexy." She shakes her little head seductively flouncing her short, coal black hair.

Mary smiles shyly, and once again is mesmerized by Rita's mystery and the privilege of being a silent but irreplaceable confidant.

Rita again fixes her eyes onto Mary. "Hans was so wonderful. I discovered uncharted realms of eroticism and intimacy with his younger, vital guidance. He was my very own guru. Of course I felt grieved when life beckoned him to move on." Rita's eyes release Mary's for a moment and ascend to the heavens in heroic self immolation. "Of course our union bore fruit, my dear, dear child, Mimi. What would I do without Mimi?"

Mary ponders this question; her large head nodding seriously.

Perhaps Rita takes Mary's silence as an indication of faltering attention and gives her an emphatic prompt. "Mary, you have no idea what I've been through. Everybody left me." She stares at Mary in indignation.

A chastised Mary nods guiltily.

Rita's eyes fill with unshed tears and shine on her fickle friend. With generous forgiveness she asks, "How are you?"

Basking in that forgiveness Mary begins talking about herself. "Well, um, Rita, some things have happened to me too." Just as she searches for the right words to describe her own losses, Rita silences her with beatific force.

"Mary, you've gone through so much. Sometimes when I was in the throes of my losses I'd look out my lonely window at the depths of the night sky. It seemed to be pulling me out of my body into its dangerous embrace, but a tiny voice inside kept calling me back, `Rita, Rita, come back, come back. You have important things to do'" She opens her large arms for a moment as if still drawn to the sky. "Oh Mary, I know it's important that we have met again."

Rita's body jerks, startling at the sound of a blaring car horn. Suddenly she looks at her own outspread arms as if they were a stranger's. Just for an instant she looks lost, and then the moment fades. She catches her bearings and nods forcefully at Mary. "Come to our little group on Tuesday."

Mary's head nods nervously.

"My teacher, a brilliant man, a prominent disciple of Milton Marcellus, leads a discussion group on getting to know your shadow self. I think he feels a very special connection to me." She smiles coyly. "This is a very special group of people, we have powers."

Although Mary's head keeps nodding, she looks away in panic.

Rita again takes the reins. "Well, it's all settled, I'll see you next Tuesday. We navigate those dark winds." Her hand invades her purse, pulling out a pencil stub and a piece of paper. Ferociously she scribbles on the paper and thrusts it into Mary's hand.

Mary's fingers tighten anxiously around the scrap of paper as Rita bolts away into the shadowy evening.

Mary shivers as if tickled by an unexpected breeze.

Chapter 4

Mary finds her way down the shadowy dead end street of her home; up ahead the house towers black in the darkness, except for a flickering light in the dining room window. Mary hears strains of spooky music seeping through an open window. She carefully unlocks the door and steps in.

Belinda, dressed in black, kneels over a bundle of burning incense sticks, smoke enveloping her body. She springs to her feet, "Well?"

Mary looks down, glancing from side to side. "Well?!"

Mary begins peering through the smoke. "There were lots of people there."

Belinda flaps her flowing sleeves impatiently, smoke stirring around her.

"Well, I got to the Convention Center all right. It was real crowded when I got in, and then a man jumped on stage and started leading everyone in some kind of prayer or something."

Belinda smiles eerily from her cloud. "And then?"

Mary looks bewildered for a moment, but brightens. "Then I saw Rita Reinke. I knew her from before....we talked outside for a while. She said I should go to this group with her."

Belinda's eyes open wide with excitement. "I told you, you needed to go!" She can barely contain herself. "What kind of group?"

Mary shakes her head. "Oh, just something about shadows."

Belinda springs out of her smoky cloud, no longer a prophetess, now an excited child. "You're going to go Mary, aren't you, aren't you?"

Mary looks down, "But..."

"Well?!" Belinda's eyes pierce Mary through the smoke.

"I don't know..."

Belinda turns away and starts humming ferociously.

Mary watches her. "I just want everything to be all right again."

Belinda transforms into a pleading child. "Please, pretty please."

Mary shrugs. "But you gotta promise me you'll go out sometime soon."

Belinda nods and sits down in her cloud of incense.

That same night as waves of terror are pounding

through Mary's paralyzed body. Try as she can, the implications of going to a meeting and being introduced to new people keep storming into her mind setting her whole body a tremble.

Chapter 5

The night before that heralded meeting, with gridlock intensity, Mary passes out hundreds of different little pills to scores of nursing home clients. No mishaps tonight, at least none that she knows of. As she walks home in the cool of that brightening summer morning her steps move forward with a certain resolution drawing her on.

By the evening she is humming a nervous melody as she says goodbye to her sister.

At 6 p.m., Belinda in a frayed, red plaid bathrobe waves goodbye to a Mary.

Walking from the refuge of her dead end street, the swell of the soft summer evening cushions Mary from overpowering dread. Crickets like a chorus of little tiny munchkins cheer her on. She catches a bus which drops her off downtown. Then she hunches in front of a shop window filled with expensive clothes on thin manikins before taking the plunge to find and catch the cross town bus. She tries to time her arrival at the meeting perfectly--a few minutes late. Not late enough to be rude of course, but late enough to save her from the task of attempting to explain herself over and over again to each newly arriving person.

She reaches her destination, a very ordinary looking house; she steps out of the bus into the unknown. As her feet touch the terra firma she frantically hunts through the chaos of her purse, scrambling to locate the little torn slip of paper on which Rita had scribbled the address. Her sweaty hand pulls out the crumpled paper; opening it up; yes, this is the right house. She freezes for a moment, her face white and rigid like a mask. Her torso suddenly jerks forward and her legs start up. She walks up to the half open door.

What should she do? Maybe this isn't the right house after all. She knows that she can get the simplest things wrong. She shakes her head; it's too late to stop now. She peers inside the door and whispers, "I don't mean to bother you, but is anybody here?"

No answer--she can't just step into a stranger's house--what would people think? She imagines herself dressed only in her underwear and closes closes her eyes. Her lips start moving slowly repeating over and over again, "I am at home in the universe. I am at home in the universe. I am at home in the universe." She opens her eyes. Is that the sound of some kind of bell ringing? This might be the right place. She takes a deep breath and resolutely totters over the threshold.

This time she speaks in a stronger more urgent voice. "Hello, hello, is anyone there?"

She hears a deep voice answering from the bowels of the house. "Come in."

With relief she follows the order, picking her way through the crowded hallway, past the strange masks on the wall watching her, past the dream catchers just waiting for the next dream. She can hear hushed voices now--yes there's a flickering light up ahead; she smells incense. Follow the light, follow the light, follow the light.

Squinting her eyes slightly, she steps toward the flickering light and into a small room with people sitting in a circle. She quickly glances at herself to make sure she has her clothes on, and then takes a quick look around.

A solemn man, gray haired, dressed in some kind of a regalia stands above a flickering light. Then she notices the other faces sitting, encircling the candle. Yes, they are smiling at her like they don't have a mean bone in their bodies, but no sign of Rita. The man raises his arms and stares intently at Mary; all the other faces follow suite.

Mary looks down whispering in a high nervous voice, "Oh, I'm sorry."

The leader smiles at her beatifically. The faces around him smile. He solemnly speaks, "Welcome dear one."

Mary glances behind her to see to whom this magnificent person is talking."

The leader speaks fixing his eyes ardently on Mary. "Welcome child of the universe." He motions gracefully at her, inviting Mary into the circle of faces.

Mary swallows as she glances at his arms. Clumsily she moves into the sacred space. She can barely get the words out. "My name is Mary Bl-,Bl-,Blu. Rita said I should…"

The leader doesn't let her finish. "Let the universe bless you, Mary Blu." The crowd of smiling people separates to leave an opening in the circle.

Tottering she sits down in the space, eyes darting around, trying to see and copy what other people are doing.

Banging sounds issue from the dark hallway. Scurrying steps rush toward the room; Rita's intense little form enters muttering, "That MIMI never leaves me alone." She shoves herself into the circle next to Mary who loses her balance and falls into the serene person sitting on her left side. A rippling wave of disturbance pulse through the circle of devotees. When the wave reaches the leader, he strikes a gong and smiles at everyone in the circle. "Welcome dear children!"

All faces, expectant as baby birds watching their mother, stare up at him.

Mary keeps nodding and smiling whispering, I'm sorry, I'm sorry".

This is the cue for which the leader has been waiting; his deep voice fills the circle as he launches into the story of his journey.

It turns out that in his previous reincarnation he had sold insurance until the fateful day in which he was driving down a highway en route to an important meeting. Up ahead he could see that the traffic was stalled. He edged his car closer nervously checking the time. In a fit of restrained rage, he stepped out of the car slamming the door viciously. A state of heightened self righteousness pushed him towards that frozen chaos. He approached. There in the very middle of the highway stood one single duck. Cars sounded their horns ferociously while voices screamed out of car windows; the duck stood immobile. That's when God spoke to him knocking him off his high horse. Entranced he walked into the center of the storm. The bird, perhaps recognizing a more familiar predator, squawked and then flew into the sky.

As The Leader now rests his brimming eyes on each and every member of his audience he says, "That duck forgot he could fly. At that very moment I realized that I had forgotten too! That's when I knew I had important things to do. I moved from Des Moines to this great city which is at the very heart of an important energy intersection. I met Julie and now at the tender age of 43, I am a new father who shares child care duties with his wife."

The audience basks in his satisfaction; at least most of them.

The din of earrings jangling disturbs the room, calling people to attention. A troubled Rita stirs.

"When I was raising my little dear, no one helped me, me." She pointed ferociously at herself.

The solemnity of the moment has been disturbed; people in the group glance anxiously at each other.

The Leader takes control with overpowering sympathy. "Rita, Rita, Rita, you've done so many courageous things in your life..." He doesn't need to finish the sentence; the whole room appears to gaze into the pool of Rita's courage. The jangling stops. Mary notices what looks like relief on people's faces.

He now continues solemnly whispering the name "Carl Jung." The leader pauses as if he is about to reveal some arcane mystery that could be dangerous to the uninitiated. "Carl embraced his shadow self, those parts of us that seem like demons; our dark nights of possibility. Of course I myself have grown immeasurably by delving into that abyss." He smiles serenely.

Mary shudders in her seat frightened at the possibility that she might have to take a little detour into the dark side before she could go directly into Oz or heaven or wherever the New Age leads; not that she really believes in anything other than her own feeble, futile attempts to delay doom. For a moment allowing herself to remember her secret medication mishaps, she sees herself tip toeing near the edge of a bottomless pit into which she refuses to look. She jerks back catching her balance and preventing a spill into some dark inevitability.

He nods slowly, whispering dramatically, "The

shadow lies in wait behind our self satisfied stories, watching for the right moment…" he pauses savoring the suspense, his voice booms, "To pounce!"

Mary gasps.

"We have no choice but to embrace the dark nights of possibility." His eyes glittering, his voice trails off in ecstasy as he whispers again, "Possibility."

Abruptly he reaches over and clicks on a bright light and is transformed into an ineffectual looking, balding middle aged man; his acolytes into a motley crew of people; not that Mary notices.

She does notice across the circle, a man and a woman sit clumped together leaning on each other. Actually the man is doing the leaning, his face drooping in melancholy while she resolutely props him up. While the woman is using all her not inconsiderable severity to prop up the larger limp man, she glances at Mary introducing herself as Mona and her husband as Henry. He says nothing as his whole body droops in some final act of resignation. Mary nods impressed by their coordination and notices the glimmer of an earring in his left ear lobe.

Resolute Mona speaks, "My Henry has just quit a very important job to explore his inner self."

Mary notices the tiniest of nods from the mysterious Henry.

The leader announces with a flourish, "Come join in our humble repast. We have stone ground, organic, blue corn, unsalted tortilla chips, and a fine selection of herbal teas." With a studied, mischievous glint in his eyes, he also announces the presence of a darker treat, chocolate chip cookies.

Almost everyone forms into a sedate cluster around The Leader. Mary tries to inconspicuously sidle her bulky form toward the table on which sits a plate of chocolate chip cookies. Whether it was his advanced psychic powers or simply Mary's imposing size, The Leader notices her and bathes his new student in attention. "Mary, I heard that you are a longtime and faithful friend of our Rita.

Mary nods compliantly as she clutches at her chocolate prize. She knows that she is supposed to speak now, "Ya, we used to know each other a long time ago." Her head bobbles up and down.

Milton nods sagely as if pondering a koan. "I feel deeply honored by your presence and hope that you will take the opportunity to share our humble but genial hospitality in the future."

Mary smiles, head still bobbing, and flees to a corner, cookie melting in her grasp. She lifts the cookie to her mouth and then glances to see if anyone is watching. Henry is staring at Mary, a strange excited smile on his face. He whispers, "Taste good?"

Mary hunches up in embarrassment.

Henry sidles closer, his face now inches away from Mary. "My name is Henry."

Mary looks up smiling shyly.

From a distance Rita watches the pair. She barges across the room standing right next to Henry. She speaks a little too loudly, "I'm on a very special, cleansing diet. Anything with sugar in it toxifies my blood." She stares at Mary ferociously. "Do you have any idea how dangerous those goddamn chocolate cookies are?"

Mary nervously crumbles the cookie in her hand.

Rita smiles at Henry and pulls out a shiny gold lipstick.

Henry stares at her humming softly.

Very slowly she applies the glossy red lipstick to her mouth.

His eyes glaze over with excitement.

Abruptly she stops, closes the lipstick and tosses it in her purse.

Henry looks bereft.

She glances at him coyly and grabs Mary by her blouse. "Let's get out of here. Have you ever been to Ray's Bar and Grill?"

Mary, who has never really been anywhere, shakes her head.

Rita glances at Henry. "There's a bartender there who has the hots for me."

Mary stuffs the cookie crumbs into her purse and lumbers after Rita.

Chapter 6

Ray's Bar is in a part of downtown that had been ignored by city developers. The bar had been the heart of a once glamorous hotel, the kind of place in which visiting celebrities used to stay. Signed photographs still line the bar walls. This collection of photographs serves as a testament to the bar's decline. Gloria Swanson, Henry Fonda, Jane Mansfield stare out from the crowded first half of the wall. Further down the wall, pictures of local weathermen, wrestlers and car salesmen are scattered more loosely. Finally the photographs disappear altogether. Now, Ray's is the kind of place that people meet for secret sometimes tawdry rendezvous: free peanuts, cheap drinks, and lights down low.

Rita pops up onto a bar stool. Mary struggles to fit her large body onto another one of those small revolving surfaces.

Rita stares at the bartender, a bored looking

middle aged man with a big stomach and a small bow tie.

He glances nonchalantly at Rita. "What can I get you?"

Rita's bravado evaporates. She looks sideways at him like a shy young girl. Even her voice becomes high pitched and coy. "Give me something pretty pink...pretty please."

The bartender fixes her with a cold stare, "A screw driver it is." He turns toward Mary, "And you?"

Mary wobbles nervously on her stool, "I, I don't really drink much."

Rita is once again a grown woman. She looks slyly at the bartender and mutters, "Give her a Virgin Mary."

The bartender glances at Rita slyly, "Another virgin coming up." He turns away and nonchalantly dumps ice into a glass over which he pours brown liquid. He shoves it across the bar towards Rita without looking up, "Screw driver it is." Then he pours blood red liquid into a glass and fiercely sticks a long spike of pickle into it. "Virgin Mary it is." He moves closer to Mary, studies her briefly and pushes the glass right in front of her.

Rita shoots a look of fierce hostility at the back of her careless suitor and starts talking at Mary again. She draws out the name, "Henry," a little too loudly with breathy relish. "Henry and Mona Mueller are dear friends of my childhood reunited with me in this New Age. He's a very, very deep man. I know in my gut that if Mona were out of the damn picture, Henry and I would be more than friends." She winks at Mary. "He and I talk about profound ideas even when Mona's there. He'd give me the shirt off his back." She pauses perhaps to relish this picture before returning to less savory topics.

The bartender watches Mary.

Rita frowns. "Mona's a therapist; she takes such good care of people. Such a devoted, practical creature; perhaps a bit too limited for Henry though. He needs someone with lots of surprises."

Mary is now unsuccessfully trying to drink her Virgin Mary without getting the pickle spike in her eye; she maneuvers the glass in front of her face.

"Someone like me, me." Rita impatiently yanks the pickle out of Mary's glass. "He needs someone with style." She grabs her lipstick out of her purse and begins carefully relining her bright red lipstick. She glances up at the bartender to see if he is watching.

He has other concerns.

Mary brings the glass of thick red liquid, unencumbered with the pickle up to her face, and quickly glances around to check if people are watching her. She presses the glass to her mouth. The coolness against her lips startles her. She takes a delicate sip; the cool thick liquid going down her throat is reassuringly comforting.

She smiles proudly at Rita, and takes a larger gulp.

Rita slaps Mary on the back. "Hasn't anybody taught you anything?"

Mary caught mid-gulp coughs, spluttering and choking uncontrollably. She spews blood red liquid over the bar.

Rita shakes her head in disbelief.

Shocked, Mary freezes, and then inching her eyes around the room, she picks up a napkin and frantically begins mopping up the bar surface.

Rita watches. "Would you stop that?" She glances resentfully at the bartender. "Fatty over there will clean that up."

Mary nods.

Rita once again smiles companionably.

Looking forlornly at the half empty glass in front of her, Mary pushes it away. "Things haven't been going so well, but…"

Rita interrupts her. "I have a mission." she closes her eyes. Even the bartender stops pouring a drink… there is a moment of stillness throughout the bar. She opens her eyes; her voice rings with a desperate urgency, "A mission…I've got to do it." She closes her eyes again. When she opens them, She flashes anger, "That goddam Mimi. She never leaves me alone." She glances at the bartender seductively. "I work for a man named Mel James. I took one look at him, and we both knew we were soul mates." She winks at Mary suggestively.

Bewildered Mary nods.

"He's got a thing for me." She smiles coyly. "He says we need a nurse, not that I can't handle everything myself..state regulations and all. Just yesterday he said he needs someone to help …She loses her train a of thought for an instant, but snaps back. "He runs his houses for craz…mentally ill people, a nurse, any kind of nurse."

Mary now glances at that abandoned pickle on the counter and shrugs her shoulders hopelessly. The word "nurse" triggers some kind of recognition. That word triggers Mary's tentative question. "I wonder if maybe…I suppose you don't…but I'm a nurse and…"

Rita smiles slyly. "Oh what the hell! For old time's sake."

Mary grabs the pickle biting off the end with satisfaction and smiles…yes the universe cares.

Rita takes command. "Call Mel tomorrow." She hastily scribbles a number on a napkin.

Mary is beginning to rock nervously on her bar stool, "but…"

A little furrow between Rita's carefully plucked eyebrows begins to flicker, "Tomorrow!" Her eyes are once again riveted onto the bartender. Without glancing at Mary she says, "See you next week."

Mary looks startled. "Next week?"

"Ya, next week!" Rita scrambles from her seat and rushes out of the bar.

Mary sits there alone for a moment, nodding.

The bartender fixes his gaze on her.

She doesn't notice as she tries to get off her unsteady perch and finally lumbers out of the bar and into the night. She has never been downtown at night before. At a shadowy corner her eyes search the darkness for dangerous, shadowy figures. Right before her panic swells up to nightmarish proportions; the bus approaches her like some unnoticed possibility and stops in front of her opening its doors.

Chapter 7

By the time Mary reaches the refuge of her home, the whole evening has become a story with which to entertain Belinda. Even the forlorn strains of Tammy Wynette singing "Stand by Your Man" soaking the house with complaint can hardly cloud Mary's new found story.

Mary interrupts Belinda who is painting birds on rocks in the living room. Ever since the untimely demise of their parents, Belinda has begun rendering images of birds startled into flight on almost every large stone in that large and stony yard.

"It was amazing, everyone was so interesting, and then Rita took me out for a drink at a bar downtown."

Belinda looks up, long enough to be reassured that her sister is home. "You're so brave Mary. I wish some day I could go out there." Then Belinda returns with feverish intensity to her labors.

Mary pauses for a second stumbling over that

caged, frantic look on her sister's face. Mary reassures her sister, "Boy Belinda, that's a beautiful bird!"

That night as Mary polishes her white shoes and carefully irons her white uniform to a crisp, she remembers the last winter, their first parentless winter in the dark endless cold of a Minnesota winter.

The snowy wind slammed into the single pane windows as the huge octopus of a furnace battled the cold. The enormous heating bills stood as testimony to its staunch determination.

Belinda looked more peeked than usual that winter as if haunted by those fuel bills that she felt so helpless to pay. Even circling employment ads in newspapers didn't help. Finally perhaps as a desperate apology, Belinda redoubled her efforts around the house: hanging pine branches from hooks on the living room ceiling, painting fleeing Canada Geese on the dining room wall, and burning stacks of incense.

That was the winter that Mary decided to do the graveyard shift at the nursing home. Not that she liked staying up at night, but things at the nursing home weren't as busy; she was less likely to make a mistake.

One early morning in that winter of discontent, Mary returned to that rattling, chilly house to find Belinda sitting in the bald, stuffed chair staring out of the window at the stubbornly frozen yard, crying. Not that crying seemed inappropriate to Mary given their circumstances; she was quick to comfort. "Oh Belinda, everything'll be all right."

That's when Belinda lifted her tearful but ecstatic

face and whispered, "Mary it was so beautiful, I saw a red cardinal perched like burning hope on the dogwood bush out there. My soul cried it was so tender."

Mary's body shudders shaking off memories, what good have they ever done. Rita's command now echoes through her mind, "Call Mel tomorrow." Other people might have time for memories, but she needs to go to bed right away to get ready for that thing that she has to do. She needs to be ready for any disaster.

Tossing in bed she keeps her anxiety at bay until the sound of her own blood frantically pumping in her ears, forces her to turn on her back, looking up into her murky future helplessly; she is so hot. A nightmare voice in her head shrieks. "What are you doing? As if things aren't bad enough you need to talk to a strange man this morning…about a job! Are you crazy?!" The voice keeps blaring in her head as the sound of pumping blood courses faster and faster in her ears. Her pillow is soaked with sweat.

In the eerie glow of the street lamp outside her window she sits up in her room and stares hopelessly at the glowing digital clock--3:00. Desperately she crawls under the covers and huddles there briefly. Then her whole body thrusts itself up in exasperation; she looks at the clock--3:15. She rubs her eyes, staring at the clock angrily. Defeat overcomes defiance as she pushes the covers down and sits up on the edge of the creaking bed on which her father had died. She stares into space.

Her left hand grabs the napkin with the frightening number scribbled on it. Mechanically she numbly dresses in her crisp whites and tiptoes down the stairs in her stocking feet, slowly stopping at every creaking sound. She doesn't want to wake Belinda.

Finally she makes it to the bottom of the stairs looking baffled, so unused is she to being out of her routine. Finally she totters over to the large dark shape of the easy chair; the chair her mother used to sit on as she stared out the front window. Mary settles into the big shadowy shape. She sits there, her left hand clasping that paper napkin on which Rita had written her order.

Three hours later Mary snores peacefully in the chair. In the window the sky is robin's egg blue. After a last snore she shutters. Her eyes spring open in surprise. She glances down at her left hand. That little bit of napkin has fallen on her lap. She stares at it; slowly her face tightens in alarm. She stands up and begins pacing the room. Finally she sits down at the mustard colored dining room table; very tentatively she picks up the phone and slowly, cautiously touches the keys all the while glancing at the napkin.

A voice filters through the telephone receiver. "Milk of Human Kindness, Mel James here."

Mary's eyes widen in terror--her body freezes. After a long pause she is able to squeak out an answer. "Um, Mel, I mean Mr. James, you don't know me."

The voice oozes sarcasm. "Swell, All I need is

the other seven billion people on earth that I don't know, to call me."

"My name is Mary Blu."

"So what."

Mary's head wobbles in determination now. "Rita said I should call."

"Is this some kind of joke?"

Mary whispers. "Rita Reinke."

"That Rita. Why didn't you tell me that in the first place?"

No answer from Mary; her whole body is wobbling now. Finally she grasps the seat of the dining room chair on which she is sitting and steadies herself. "Rita said you might have some kind of job…I mean working with Rita."

"So that's what Rita said."

Mary echoes back, "That's what Rita said."

"Can you do anything else besides wasting people's time on the phone?"

Mary freezes again. Upstairs the floor in Belinda's bedroom creaks. This rouses Mary. "You mean what I do? Ah, ah, well, I am a licenses practical nurse, at least sort of…I mean I am."

This time Mel pauses. "I could use one of those."

"You, you mean…"

"I'll see you in exactly one hour, 1018 Riverside Place." He hangs up.

As Mary listens to the dial tone muttering, "What if…" and gently puts the receiver down.

Just before she before she leaves the house, she

dials Rita's number, just to make sure that all this is happening and happening to her, Mary Blu. She hears the phone ring three times, and then the receiver being lifted in silence. "Um this is Mary Blu and I'm calling for Rita; is any one there?"

More silence.

"Um..."

A tiny voice speaks on the other end of the line. "My name's Mimi, and my mommy isn't here now."

Mary warms up to that innocent voice. "I'm so glad to meet you. Your mother has told me so many nice things about you."

"She has?"

"Oh yes--such a sweet girl."

"I am?"

"Oh yes!"

Once again there is silence on the other end of the line.

"By any chance will your mommy be home later?"

After another long pause, "Maybe."

"Would you tell her that her old friend Mary Blu called?" "

"She doesn't have any friends."

Mary heard the receiver slam down.

Mary keeps talking. "Everything is going to be all right." Slowly she puts the receiver down.

Chapter 8

Once again Mary sets off, up that dead end street, and takes a bus to an unknown destination. She only has to remind the bus driver once about her destination.

She steps out of the bus and into a neighborhood of large old decaying houses. At the turn of the Twentieth Century this street had been a showcase of wealth, each house outdoing the other with imposing extravagance. Ninety years later, the imposing front porches are sagging, turrets are boarded up, and grandeur has been subdivided into shoddy little apartments. Lost looking listless people wander the sidewalks.

Mary hopes that she, for once in her life is prepared, holding the bit of paper with address wadded up in her hand. She spreads the crinkled paper across her palm, glances up at the address on the towering houses around her and with a semblance of determination walks toward a severe looking three story red brick house. A large brick arch frames the entrance. Once there must have been an equally grand door, but now a peeling wooden wall closes off that entrance. Set in that doorway is a plain metal door. Above it hangs a sign, "The Milk of Human Kindness." Mary presses the doorbell that has been installed at a slightly crooked angle.

She waits at that entrance, her left hand crunching that wadded piece of paper. Finally she hears shuffling footsteps on the other side of the door. The door opens hesitantly; a young woman, wild eyed, stares out blinking desperately as if day were an alien environment. She whispers to Mary, "Do you belong here?"

Maybe it was those trips Mary had been taking of late, or maybe just that the person answering the door seemed like some woodland creature, frightened and exposed, Mary says, "yes."

The wild eyed woman stares out the door suspiciously for a moment. Her face softens. "My name is Teresa. Have you come to live here?"

Mary ponders this question. "I might come to work here. I talked with Mel James. Do you know who is?"

Teresa's eyes glance back into the hallway suspiciously.

"I think maybe he's the one who is in charge here."

Teresa hopelessly nods at Mary and then turns around shuffling down the narrow dark hallway.

Mary follows.

At the end of the hallway is a gray wall; set in the wall is a grand door, perhaps the same door that once graced the front of the building. Teresa nods toward the door with resignation and flees back down the hallway.

A large bronze plaque is screwed to the door. On it is etched "Mr. Melvin James." Mary studies that name, even running her fingers over the groves of the letters. She takes a deep breath and knocks softly at the door--silence. She shuffles from foot to foot.

Then through the door she hears a voice demand, "Knock louder!"

Mary pounds more loudly on the door.

From the other side of the door she hears a voice yell, "Not that loud! What do you think this is?"

Mary stands numbly at the door.

"Well are you going to come in or just stand out there all day?"

Mary's hand clutches the bronze door knob and slowly turns it. As she pushes the door open wide open, light explodes into her face. Squinting she can see a dark figure in the center of that brilliant explosion. As Mary pieces her shattered vision together she can make out a huge desk behind which sits a shadowy silhouette. Brilliant daylight floods into the stuffy room from the floor length glass wall behind the figure. At this point Mary realizes that she is hot, very hot.

The figure stands up, a tall, sinuous shape of a

man stretching, basking in the warm light. Small bright darting eyes shine out from the dark shape. As her eyes begin to get used to the light, Mary notices one glistening drop of sweat run down his partially exposed chest. She blushes.

"What did you say your name is?" He slithers back into his chair.

"Mary, Mary Blu."

He hisses, "Why are you bothering me?"

"I, um, just thought I had an appointment with you." She can feel her once crisp uniform begin to dampen and cling to her torso.

"You're Rita's friend. How is the old gal? Do you think she's going to make it?"

"Ah, make what?"

"Well, well, never mind." Mel grins and looks her up and down in calculating appraisal as she stands squirming in the overheated room. "You gotta do what you are told. You got your work; I have mine."

Mary gulps, her head nodding uncontrollably. "I always try my best to do what I am told."

Mel smiles with satisfaction. "That a girl--report to Rita what's her name next Monday."

Mary stands up awkwardly, her rumpled uniform sticking to her sweaty body. "This means a lot to…"

"What are you wasting my time for now?"

Chapter 9

"I'm involved with something mysterious, profound, something even large enough for the breath and depth of my vision...a mission." Rita interrupts her focus on the bartender long enough to be assured that the implications of this revelation are dawning on Mary.

So many changes, Mary's life keeps moving faster and faster, Rita, the driving force in this chaos. Mary nods her head reassuringly as Rita talks, a small price to pay for the breath of air filtering through the confines of Mary's life. Rita's eyes stare at Mary demanding her attention. Mary's head bobs in attention as Rita, eyes glittering, begins telling her story.

"I was doing a wonderful job at that little library; after all I was in complete charge. With my charm and vision I was able to motivate all those little people under me. Of course occasionally someone got out of line but I fuckin' showed them." She pauses disoriented for a moment as if straddling two diverging stories.

She chooses the more placid mount and continues. "I knew that though I was doing important work something more awaited me, beckoning in the distance, something with broader scope that might even encompass the world!" Her bold little body vibrates in excitement. "That's when I met Glen. At exactly 1PM every Wednesday he would open the door of the library and peek in to see if there were any empty tables. After carefully reconnoitering he'd pick out the most recent newspaper, sit down, and within minutes be holding a muffled but animated conversation with himself. His voice scratched across the silence of my library. First I tried to charm him into quiet submission and then I tried a more emphatic approach. But he just wasn't concerned. That was about the time I lost Hans, the love of my life. I suddenly realized that Glen was a very a mysterious and important person.

I now waited for him. On Wednesdays I would stop my cataloging and wouldn't even answer phones. Like clockwork he'd step into the library on his mission, on our mission. For the next two hours I would immerse myself in that deep wild river of his wisdom, bathing in freedom and light. Between my astrologer and Glen I began to see that all my brilliant organizing was simply a foreshadowing of the awesome pattern the cosmos was now revealing to me.

I started to use my little library to express this

truer order of things. I bought loads of shinny silver paste-on stars and gave them out to all the customers telling them to stick those little buggers on any page of their books that spoke to them with cosmic meaning. The kids loved it, and sometimes I'd have lines of them just waiting to get their boxes of stars. Every Wednesday morning I would lead the staff and everyone else present in our Dance of the Universe. I'd say, `Twinkle now, everybody twinkle!' Of course most of the staff were stick-in-the-muds and I was about to fire the whole goddamn lot of them when the district supervisor dropped in. He wouldn't twinkle either.

I didn't work for a while after that. I just kept listening to that twinkling music all around me."

For a moment all grandeur drained from Rita's eyes and she looked up at Mary's solid form for solace. Then Rita, refreshed by Mary's devotion, took a drink of her screw driver and charged on. "Mimi was my only companion during all those years. Sometimes she would even talk on the phone for me if I was too busy listening to the stars. She was the one who found the want ad that day. Of course she never lets me forget that, the bitch." Once again Rita lost her train of thought. She shook her head and with determination caught a ride on the smoother train again. "Mimi's little hand was trembling as she showed me the paper. There it was, a message meant just for me: 'Wanted, a first rate supervisor, looking for life purpose working with mentally challenged people. Ask for Mel James, an equal opportunity employer.'"

"I knew immediately that Mel had a mission too. The rest is history. Mel took one look at me and hired me on the spot. He must have recognized a kindred soul."

Perhaps Mary is only imagining it, but she thinks that she too can hear the distant sound of something like twinkling and just for a moment dares to think that she might have a place in some grand scheme.

As if sensing Mary's fledgling enthusiasm, dry little wisps of Rita's black hair begin dancing with electricity. "I ran into you for a reason, Mary, a powerfully, deep reason. I need a second in command. My responsibilities are increasing so rapidly, I could use some one like you, someone who is...a real nurse."

From some deep hidden pool of excitement, waves begin pulsing through Mary's large form. Each mounting wave drives her nearer to a chasm across which she has never ventured. With a tickling explosion, she reaches the summit and can just make out a panorama of far off possibilities.

Just as she is about to coast into hope, she jolts to a stop, lashed back in panic...a father gasping for breath, a mother lying dead and cold in a urine soaked bed, medications just waiting to be given to the wrong person, and something hiding and painful inside Belinda. Mary's eyes open in a frightened stare, her whole large form totters as if absorbing a shock that explodes inside her. She steadies herself on the chair, gathering the bits of herself. Then she remembers that duck she heard about at the Shadow Group. Perhaps she too has forgotten how to fly; she nods at Rita. "I think maybe I should do it, I do, I think I really do. We worked together once, and I'll just do it again!"

Rita snaps her attention from the bartender and again pins her companion down with her gaze. "Mary, you won't goddamn regret this. This job has your name written all over it."

Before Mary has a chance to say that maybe everything is happening a little too fast, Rita wrestles up her purse and rushes toward the door. "Call me tomorrow. See you at work, Monday."

"Sure Rita, sure."

Much more tentatively Mary follows in Rita's wake out of the bar. She just hopes that Belinda will understand. Mary paces at the dark bus stop, not even caring if a dangerous stranger lurks in the shadows.

The bus pulls up; Mary shakes her head wondering to what destination her life is traveling. True when she left the house this evening for a second visit with the Shadow Group and Rita, Belinda had been igniting a whole bundle of incense sticks, filling the house with billowing smoke that would have set off the fire alarm if Belinda hadn't figured out how to turn it off. Mary enters the door of that dead end house more carefully than usual, now trying to remember why she was changing jobs. Belinda's plaid bath-robed form sits engulfed in billowing smoke in the middle of the living room, coughing as she peers at the glowing incense sticks all carefully stuck in a pile of sand. She looks up at Mary, divining that something terrible is about to happen.

Mary looks at her sister almost slyly. "Oh, hi Belinda, it's nice of you to wait up for me. Is that some of that new incense; it smells so nice?"

Belinda silently glances up through the narrowed slits of her eyes.

Mary stumbles ahead, "I've got some good news. I know you're going to like it. Things will be so much better for us. You'll be just fine; I'll make sure of that."

Belinda now stares at her in wounded accusation. "Mary, what's happening? What are you doing now?"

Guilt now overcoming her new found slyness, Mary looks down. "I just want to tell you that I'm getting a better job so we'll be safer."

"Safer? You said that the last time and look what happened to mom and dad."

"You'll see everything will be all right, Belinda. You'll see." Mary studies her sister's unforgiving face.

Chapter 10

The next day Mary phones Rita. "I just wanted to call to see if you still want me…you know…"

Rita whispers, "Henry is such a deep man. I attract men like that. He started to work for me two weeks ago. Of course you realize that he's just waiting for a really important job that fits his extraordinary talents. He is one of my fleet of valiant people who go out and visit mentally ill people. That's what Mel's company does. Some of those dear people live in houses that he provides. Some of the others live in regular apartments. Mel pays people to visit them. For Henry though, it's pocket money. Just the other day, Mary Lou Arndte, a delusional client called me and said, 'Thank God, thank God for the wonder of Henry.' I was deeply touched to see my mission being so wonderfully accomplished."

Mary hears heavy breathing and rustling and then a new voice comes through the receiver.

"Is this my mommy's friend Mary?"

Mary pauses for a moment, not so much to consider the question, because after all she really knows her name is Mary, but rather to anticipate the needs of this new person. Besides, Mary doesn't really know how to handle sudden transitions. Anything with movement, particularly unexpected movement is a challenge for her. As she stares into space, she suddenly realizes that this voice belongs to Mimi, why of course it is Mimi. Mary's voice becomes ever so sweet. "Is this Mimi?"

"Oh Mary don't be a silly. Of course it's me, me.

Mary smiles with the unexpected satisfaction of being right. "You sound like such a sweet little girl. I sure hope I get a chance to meet you."

"Don't worry about that Mary. Mommy has plans for you. We'll be seeing lots of you."

Again a dull wrestling sound fills the receiver.

Finally, Rita's more familiar voice forces its way through the receiver. "Mary, what was I saying? Oh, yah, go to 233 Groveland on Monday. It's right next to the main building."

Mary caught the change more quickly this time. "Rita thanks for the directions and letting me talk to Mimi."

"Mimi! That God damned kid won't leave me alone...fucking Mimi keeps interrupting me. She thinks she can take over whenever she wants." There is another rustling pause. It's still Rita's voice, but now she is whispering again. "Mary dear, I'm so glad

you'll be joining our little family; see you Monday…
God damn it Mimi!"…click.

Mary leaves her dangerous job at the nursing
home and begins her work with The Milk of Human
Kindness (MIHUK, to people in the business). She
reports for work that first day ready to stumble into
the demands of her new job. On the door to this much
less imposing ramshackle building is taped a piece
of paper. "Come right in. Keep turning to the left."

Mary gingerly pushes the door further open and
slips into the building. "Keep turning to the left"
echoes through her mind. First left--she turns, second
left--she turns. She hears a faint throbbing, gushing
sound coming from her left around the next corner.
She follows the sound, and across a wide empty room
sees an alcove. The loud rhythmic, gushing sound
issues from somewhere within the alcove. She tip
toes across the room and peeks into the shadowy
alcove. The walls are decorated with pictures of wolves
turning into American Indians and paintings of
ethereal female figures frolicking in amethyst castles.
Dangling off all available surfaces are plants; not just
any plants, though. These are innocent looking but
aggressive spider plants bushing out lushly, apparently
self contained, only to quietly send out long spiny
arms depositing miniature copies of themselves on
any receptive surface unfortunate enough to be in
their vicinity.

The gushing sound now loudly pulses through
Mary's brain. The sound seems to come from a black

box sitting on the floor next to a large desk across which a very small Rita whose glittering eyes peer at Mary with mysterious expectation.

"At last!" Rita whispers solemnly.

Mary's head bobbles and finally nods.

Rita stands up behind her desk. "This is it, my domain." Rita's large right hand motions to a small desk, piled high with papers just outside the alcove. "That's your desk."

"What a nice…" Mary doesn't move but stands there fascinated by her surroundings. She notices shiny stars scattered across Rita's desk. "My sister would like your desk; she's so artistic."

"Would you go to your goddam desk?!"

Mary slinks toward her small desk. Once seated, she finally musters the courage to ask. "What would you like me to do?"

In the distance a siren screeches. Rita suddenly jumps up and grabs her leather shoulder bag and frantically grabs a small pink case on her desk, the kind of case a small girl might use for childish cosmetics, and shoves it into her bag. She is rocking ever so slightly. She whispers urgently, "I gotta get out of here!" The sound of the siren fades into the gushing sound coming out of the black box. She caresses the little pink box. "Be right back, got some business. You know what to do." Rita charges out of the room.

Bewildered Mary paces back and forth across the room. A phone rings. It takes her a few minutes to realize that the phone is on her desk. Hesitantly she picks up the receiver.

"Is this Rita's friend Mary?"

Mary struggles for her bearings. "Yes, but who…"

"Don't be such a silly. You know who I am. I'm Mimi."

Mary has found her bearings now. "What a sweet little voice you have. I sure hope I get a chance to meet you."

"Don't worry about that Mary. Will you take care of me?"

"Oh yes."

"Bye, bye Mary."

"Good bye Mi…." the dial tone buzzes through the receiver. For the next 10 minutes Mary dutifully sits at her desk, occasionally squirming uncomfortably.

Rita finally rushes back into the office and into her alcove. She silently and obliviously sits behind her desk.

Mary watches Rita for some kind of sense of direction. Her head starts bobbling nervously. "Maybe there is something that you want me to do?"

Without looking up, Rita glances toward the black box out of which issues the strange rhythmic slushing sound. "That's the sound of my heart beating. I recorded it."

Mary pauses for a moment then in a tiny voice says, "That's the sound of your…?"

Rita commands, "YOU have work to do!"

Mary starts fumbling through the papers piled on her desk.

Finally at 11 AM, Rita announces, "Time for lunch. We got a lot done this morning. I want all my employees to catch my rhythm." She jumps up from her seat and rushes out of the room. "You're coming!"

Mary stands up from her chair and lumbers after Rita.

Lunch at a greasy smelling diner down the block- -Mary timidly speaks up. "I still don't completely understand what I am supposed to…"

"You're there when I need you."

"Oh."

Those next weeks, Mary, sitting at a desk just outside of Rita's sanctuary, becomes the high priestess of this diminutive but potent deity. Attired in nursing whites, Mary screens supplicants with a hushed voice. "Ahhh, you're here to see Rita. Let me see if she can be interrupted." When Rita isn't there, which is often, Mary has a battery of important sounding reasons for these absences. Mary begins to feel competent even though she still doesn't understand the exact extent of her duties.

There is a period of months during which Mary almost smells land. Best of all, she doesn't have to pass out medications; any mistakes she makes now are intangible and beyond her consideration. For Mary that machine of her destiny driven by some hidden flaw, seems to slow down. That autumn she notices the high honking sound of geese flying south and the way squirrels bury acorns in any loose soil. Rita who is rather vague about her own hours is nonchalant but nevertheless pleased with Mary's timeliness.

When Rita actually occupies her sacred space, even the inhabitants of the upstairs offices become strangely restless, out of excitement or apprehension. Once while Rita is out, Mary peeks into that inner sanctum, exploring hesitantly. She even stares at the little pink box that Rita has left behind on the desk.

Perhaps it is Mary's burgeoning sense of safety, but one day…"Um Rita, I know it's not important and probably not any of my business, but I wonder what that little pink box is for? If you were out or something maybe I might need to know?"

Rita's face scrunches up; she glares at Mary with fierce defiance.

Mary watches. Maybe it was the sound of geese honking… she realizes that Rita's face has a way of changing, a bit like the horse of many colors that Dorothy saw when she entered into the Land of Oz.

"That goddam pink box is the center of all my systems. It's very, very important and very, very private!"

"I just thought…" Her voice trails off.

"Leave it the fuck alone!"

One particularly gloomy day in late November, the world frozen an inert gray, Henry, mysteriously bundled in a trench coat, rushes into Rita's office silently past Mary. A few minutes later he leaves as secretly as he came.

Like a sly conspirator Rita slips out of her luxuriant bower to speak with Mary. "Mary, I've just spoken with Henry. What a deep man!" She pauses for a minute to let Mary bathe in the implications of Henry's name. "He mentioned, of course this is off the record, that in his spiritual journey he has uncovered an urgent need for platonic, female friendship. Though for romantic purposes, he prefers daintier women; she flounces her black pixie hair. "I suggested that you might fit the bill. Possibly, just possibly you may be getting a little call from him."

Chapter 11

That very evening, Mary clangs around the drab old fashioned kitchen. Her feet shuffle back and forth along a black worn pathway on the old linoleum floor. She delicately pulls out a box of macaroni and cheese from the cupboard and fumbles to open it. There--she has done it. With a certain sense of satisfaction she pours the noodles into a pan of boiling water on the stove. She watches it bubble with innocent intensity.

Minutes later she walks to the old wooden stairway and peeks up those stairs. "I'm fixing your favorite dinner, Belinda."

The sound of a door opening upstairs, reluctant footsteps

creak down the stairs.

Mary pours a packet of garish yellow powder into the noodles. She contentedly stirs the gooey yellow mess inside the pot.

Dejectedly Belinda sits down at the table.

Mary proudly heaps the yellow goo onto Belinda's plate. "That Rita is so nice to me."

Belinda stares at her plate forlornly.

"I'm not quite sure what..."

Belinda stares at Mary in disbelief. "This isn't like mom used to make!"

"Everything is going to be all r..."

Belinda throws her silverware down and rushes upstairs.

The phone rings in the other room. Mary is staring off into space. Finally reluctantly she lumbers to the phone and picks it up.

A tiny voice on the other end says, "It's me, me."

Mary looks bewildered.

"It's me silly, Mimi."

"Mimi, oh, I didn't recognize your..."

"Mommy says to be very careful about Henry. He's mommy's special friend."

Mary continues to look bewildered.

Mimi's voice grows in volume. "Do you hear me Mary?"

"I guess..."

The phone hangs up on the other end. Mary stares into the black window.

On cue, the next morning, Saturday at 9:00 AM, Mary receives a call.

"Mary!"

"Hi, who is this?"

"Henry."

"I didn't recognize your voice. I suppose I've never heard your voice much anyway..."

"I'll be by in twenty minutes."...click.

9:05 AM--Mary attempting to look like a good sport settles for a plaid shirt that had once belonged to her father and a no nonsense navy blue skirt. Carefully remembering to brush her teeth; up on the lowers and down on the uppers, by 9:15 she is tiptoeing down those creaky stares, ensuring Belinda a few more minutes of oblivion.

9:20, a large rumbling 1980 Oldsmobile station wagon pauses in front of that shabby house. Mary slips out of the door and into the trembling car.

"Hi Henry."

"Hi."

"It sure was nice of you to give me a call."

"Yeah." Henry guns the engine, and together they take off.

Mary, sitting in the presence of mysterious Henry and embarking on an even more mysterious adventure, maintains a respectful silence.

9:30, the car comes to a definite halt in front of a former gas station now the frayed but chic home of Shoe Fly, an urban experience for the young at heart. Henry steps out of the car; Mary follows suite. As she walks behind him, she notices something new about Henry; a little brown pony tail hangs down from the back of his head.

They sit down at a table with a scrabble board in the middle and place mats torn from comic books on each side. A tall, slim woman dressed in black leotards and a grimy sweat shirt stations herself in front of their table armed with a tablet and pencil.

Henry eyes her with hungry intensity. "Hey, babe, gimme the usual."

Puzzled, she rouses from her indifference long enough to say, "I'll give you coffee, eggs, and hash browns." She points her attention to Mary, "I suppose you want something too."

"Oh, thanks, I guess I'll have the same, it sounds so good."

The waitress takes one cool sip of Henry's attention and departs to grace another table.

Henry slumps down into his chair spreading his legs to take up most of the space under the table. "I hang out here."

Mary carefully places her large feet precisely under her chair, not wanting to disturb Henry's comfort. "So you come here a lot Henry?"

Henry nods, opening and closing his mouth softly.

Mary thinks about those salamanders she used to be so crazy about when she was a kid. They lurked in the moist dark window wells of her childhood. She spent many a summer morning peeking into basement window wells by houses all over the neighborhood. When she finally found a salamander she would gently pick it up by its silky middle and while its four soft feet squirmed, she would stare at it face to face, only inches apart. That's when the salamander usually opened its soft, floppy mouth and closed it again. This action signaled her to delicately place the creature back into its damp home--she realizes that she likes Henry.

The sweat-shirted waitress slamming two cups of coffee onto the table triggers Henry into speaking. "When I was in 'Nam, things happened to me. People wonder sometimes if I feel strongly about anything."

Mary sits, transfixed by the vulnerability of that slack, innocent face.

"One day about half way through my tour of duty, my platoon unexpectedly came upon a village in enemy territory. The sergeant ordered the villagers to stand up against a wall. Then he told us to gun them down. I turned to him and said, 'I can't do that.'"

Mary feels the heat of the warm cup of coffee penetrate her hand. Henry's courage subtly enters her consciousness, a growing mounting warmth. She relaxes and her body is washed in a flood of gratitude. "Henry, you really did that for all those poor people. You're a hero Henry, you really are!"

Henry smiles back his mouth opening and closing silently, leaving the rest of the breakfast conversation to Mary's halting but reassuring admiration. In the ensuing weeks Henry's presence fleeting past her at work makes her feel somehow, well, tender.

Chapter 12

Mel, basking in his deluxe, hot office begins slithering restlessly on his black vinyl chair; his normal lizard like contentment clearly disturbed. Something is wrong. He focuses on a computer screen filled with numbers and then grimaces. His darting head pauses as his eyes blink sharply and mechanically. He switches the computer screen off and picks up his phone. "Mary, how are you? I was calling to see how you're doing in our little company.'

Alone in the office Mary's voice falters, finally she says, "Thanks for..."

Mel spits out, "Come over to see me... right now!"

Mary carefully places the phone back on the receiver. Like a prisoner sentenced, she pushes herself up off her chair.

She knocks hesitantly on that huge door.

"Come in!"

Mary does.

Though the window behind him is filled with a cold gray sky webbed with barren tree branches, a large space heater glows emitting waves of heat into the enclosed room. Mel, a cold smile on his face, sits at his desk holding up a large manila envelope. He fixes his eyes on Mary as she sits down on the warm leather chair. He opens the envelope and dumps a torrent of colored glittery fragments on his desk. "What are these Mary?"

She bends over toward his desk examining the glittering bits. She frowns, "I think, well I think they might be stars."

Mel stares her down. "Brilliant, you're such a brilliant person, a credit to your profession."

Mary looks down in embarrassment.

Mel's face flashes in anger. "I asked for a report from Rita yesterday, and this is what I get!" He pounds the desk, and the glittering stars scatter.

Mary looks away.

"Mary, Mary, Mary." His voice is softening. "Next month the state is coming in. Do you know what that means?"

Mary glances up at him and shakes her head.

"If you don't have your files in order and all the forms filled out; his voice hisses out in rage, "They chew your ass out. And after they have their little lunch, they start looking at things VERY closely."

His voice softens again. "Do you want them to look closely Mary?"

Mary sits there frozen.

Mel shakes his head.

Mary shakes her head now.

"Certainly a bright, charming woman like you must notice some difficulties down there. Maybe you can even fix the problem. No one is indispensable."

He switches his computer screen on and once again begins examining the screen as if no one else were in the room.

Mary stands up bewildered. Once outside the office she pauses with a worried look on her face and then trudges back into the building that houses her tiny desk and the more life compatible atmosphere of Rita's office. Rita's wiry form once again sits embedded in the hanging plants, a serene smile peeking out from her black, pixie bangs.

It was then that Mary makes the first mistake on her new job; instead of giving reassurance, she asks for it. "Rita, something kind of strange just happened. Mel called me into his office."

Rita looks through the spider plant leaves, something darker beginning to cloud that small countenance. "Why didn't you tell me before you went to see him?!"

Mary, memory not a strong point, begins puzzling together the answer to that urgent question. Finally she has it. "Well, ah, you were probably busy somewhere else…you weren't here. That's when Mel told me to come over."

The rain forest of Rita's office begins rumbling. "What did he say to you, goddamn it?!"

Mary begins remorsefully confessing every detail of the encounter.

Rita springs up from her chair eyes flashing. "Don't you ever, fucking ever, see him again without telling me!"

Mary's head bobbles.

This signals the beginning of the battle of the titans, Rita and Mel, two forces of nature struggling for the control of an empire that contains Mary's hopes.

Mel begins showing up at Mary's desk, well before Rita arrives. Very quickly Mel brushes off Mary's practiced excuses for Rita's absence. He gets to the meat of the dilemma right away, firing a vast array of procedural questions at Mary. Fortunately she is as mystified as Mel about the inner workings of Rita's mysterious domain. She is very careful not to mention anything about that little pink box.

Mary does not inform Rita of these not so informative "tete- a-tetes."

Mel initiates a new course of action: he calls Rita several times a day with pointed questions.

That little vertical crease between her eye brows begins flickering all the time now.

Their conversations now alternate between coyness and outrage. Rita begins pacing like a wounded lioness muttering, "He's evil; he's got to be stopped!" At times she fists her large hands and almost bursts with barely contained rage. Her bangs, electrified, dance on her forehead. With that little crease between her brows flickering she throws an angry glance at Mary, muttering, "You're the one who started all this."

Mary begins preparing for exile, after all her indiscretion with Mel has triggered this unwinding tragedy. Her volatile sense of self incriminating doom is reactivated. This time, though, perhaps due to her months of relative safety, there is a brief moment of self-reflection before self-immolation; she begins wondering what her heroine Dorothy from the *Wizard of Oz* would do in this dilemma. Perhaps Mary should run away from home with her little dog Toto, but she doesn't have a dog and besides who would take care of Belinda? Then she has it--she will become a stewardess flying every day over that rainbow. With precision and charm she would wend her delicate way through those narrow aisles smiling, simultaneously pouring steaming coffee, quieting frantic babies, and yes, innocently fending off the advances of fascinated passengers. As she accidentally spills an entire pot of coffee in the lap of that sensitive and attractive single businessman from Cincinnati, she returns to the reality of her situation with Rita. Rita needs help and she, Mary, can give it. She stands up to be counted.

Not that it's easy. In spite of the taint of suspicion that settles on Mary, Rita now needs her as a bastion of support. Mary does what she has always done best, give reassurance; although Rita has definite ideas about the kind of reassurance that she wants. With some slight prodding Mary rises to the challenge.

Rita appears increasingly satisfied with Mary's performance and starts repeating, "I know Mel is up to something evil; we'll goddamn stop him!" Mary feels flattered by the inclusion and begins steeling herself for the possibility of an uncharacteristic, active role.

Chapter 13

Mary really had not thought much about the idea of mental illness before reentering Rita's dramatic orbit. Sure, she saw "The Three Faces of Eve," but she forgot who starred in it. Then there was the "Snake Pit" with her favorite 1950's actress, Olivia de Havilland. No matter how beset by the horrors of the mental hospital, Olivia maintained a certain poignant glamour.

Mostly though, for Mary, mental illness seemed like shadowy doom awaiting some people. She maintained a strained cheeriness that she hoped would mark her as normal, signaling that dark angel to pass and strike someone else. As for Belinda, well, artists were supposed to be unusual. Besides, Belinda had Mary to watch over her.

Not that Mary's role as protectoress was always easy. Just the other day when she slipped back into that dean end house, Mary noticed the corner of a book sticking out from underneath a cushion of the sofa. She pulled it out carefully. Her jaws fused together with a click and her head began to wobble- -the book was new, brand new. Belinda was a reader. Unfortunately due to her home bound status those book club brochures that came in the mail were more than tempting.

Book in hand Mary began a long and difficult journey up the stairs to Belinda's room. Every couple of feet she would stop, hunch her shoulders and gesture helplessly with her free hand. Then her feet would catch a military rhythm and carry her a little closer to the ordeal of a confrontation. Her feet could carry her no further than the open doorway of her sister's room. Mary's large mass loomed in that doorway while Belinda painted a large, flying, purple bird on the west wall of her bedroom.

Apologetically Mary squeaked out, "What a wonderful bird, Belinda."

Belinda looked up excited until she noticed the book resting like an accusation in Mary's grasp. Wildness flashed in Belinda's face.

Mary now wished she had never seen that book. She tried to erase these last five minutes, but she kept finding herself in the same doorway holding the same book. She was trapped; she had to go ahead. "Well, ah, Belinda, I saw a new book downstairs. I, ah, just wanted to remind you that you, ah, probably shouldn't join another book club. We just can't afford it, I think." Her smile twisted into an apology.

Belinda looked down guiltily, "I just couldn't help it Mary. I thought I'd try to help you with that new job of yours. This book club is a psychology book club and I'm learning all sorts of new things."

The dark mass of Mary's body began softening, reaching out to her sister. "Gee thanks Belinda, you're such a good sister. I really appreciate your help, but I'd sure like it if you wouldn't join any more of those clubs." Then Belinda's thin form began stiffening, "Oh Mary, you worry too much."

In a last stand of determination Mary pleaded "You'll keep your promise this time, won't you Belinda?"

"Mary! You don't even trust me." Belinda hit the wall with her dripping brush and left a long purple splash. "Now look what you made me do!"

Mary's head bobbed frantically. She retreated down the stairs to threw supper together.

Meanwhile back at TMOHK Henry has given up his foray into platonic female companionship, at least with Mary. After that fateful Saturday breakfast he resumes rushing past Mary en route to hushed conferences with the daintier Rita. She does notice that Henry is allowing that ponytail to grow longer and longer.

Mary isn't really offended by Henry's indifference; in fact she feels that she has a kind of honorary membership in Rita and Henry's club. Besides Rita passes along tantalizing bits of information about the romantic enigma known as Henry--he appears to be straying from the perhaps too tight grip of Mona.

Chapter 14

Back at the center of the storm Rita begins anointing every niche in her office with patchouli oil and playing a tape called *The Serenade of the Killer Whales*. The whole building fills with the cloying smell and shakes with the eerie strains of lonely but dangerous whales communicating to each other in a deep ocean.

One May afternoon, the lushness of Rita's office drawing the world into fertile abundance, Mary germinates an idea; she actually decides to share it. As Rita paces back and forth muttering, Mary apologetically catches Rita's thrashing attention. "Rita, um, I wonder if maybe you and I could sort of set up our own business? With your experience and my, um, persistence, I bet we might be able to do this business ourselves, maybe?"

Rita beleaguered by the possibility of ideas coming from anyone but herself, stares at Mary incredulously, that little vertical line between her eyebrows creasing dangerously deeper. "No, we can't! This is a damn complicated business. I can't get anything going until Mel gets off my goddam back!"

Mary looks even more reassuringly apologetic, but there is just a hint of something like sly defiance in her eyes. Thanks to Mel's distracting influence on Rita, Mary is beginning to get a very tentative sense of how the business works.

At the end of that day, shortly after Rita and Mel simultaneously hang up on each other, that wailing music and patchouli oil finally pay off.

"Mary, I've have a wonderful idea. We'll start our own business! With my experience and vision and your...I know we can do it!"

Mary listens. At first she frowns then something like sly surprise masks her face. "Oh Rita. Do you think...do you think we can?"

Catherine the Great couldn't have looked more courageous, addressing thousands of hussars, than Rita with her pliant soldier. "We can do it. After all, I know just about everything there is to know with this business. The only thing I need to come up with is someone to do the accounting." She pauses as if bewildered for a moment. "That's what fucking Mel does."

Mary smiles, plowing back into her list of things to do.

Saturday morning Mary receives another cryptic call from Henry, this time unheralded.

"Mary."

"Hi, this must be Henry; I'm starting to recognize your voice."

"Ya."

"Nice to hear from you. How are you and Mona… oops…I guess I shouldn't have asked that."

"Ya, I'll be by in twenty minutes"…click.

Teeth brushed and journey down those creaky stairs completed on tip toe, Mary exits the house and enters that rumbling station wagon that seems to be sympathetically deteriorating as fast as his suburban marriage.

"Hi, Henry."

"Hi."

"It was sure nice of you to give me a call."

"Ya." He guns the increasingly fitful engine, and together they zoom off. After an uneasy silence the car comes to a sudden halt in front of Shoe Fly.

Henry steps out of the car blankly; Mary follows suite. As Mary walks behind him she notices that Henry's lengthening ponytail is died golden blond with a turquoise colored feather attached to the end. They sit at the scrabble boarded table. A tall sensuous young man in tight black jeans and a Hawaiian shirt offers himself to Henry, ready for orders. He eyes Henry's suburban substance with soft yearning.

Henry smiles. "Hey babe, gimme the regular."

"I'll give you anything you want." Then the waiter throws a glance at Mary. "I suppose you want something too."

"Oh sure, I'll take the same. Thanks for asking."

The waiter relinquishes his pose and leaves.

"I hang out here all the time…great place."

Mary nods. "So you come here a lot Henry--what a nice place."

Henry opens and closes his mouth softly. He has a new interest. While they are both sipping their coffees, he casually lifts a rather professional looking brief case onto the table. "I was down at the library this week, brushing up on tax laws. I was thinking of starting a dry cleaning business, but I don't have enough capital." Restrained sadness filters through that slack face.

Ever eager to boost anyone else's morale, Mary says, "Henry do you know how to do all that complicated accounting stuff?"

Henry courageously breaks through the barrier of his modesty. "In my job at Systems Unlimited, I trouble shot the whole accounting department."

As Mary stares into the steam of her coffee cup, an idea dawns in her increasingly resourceful mind. Henry, with his flexible but steely integrity and his accounting experience would make an ideal third partner for Rita and maybe herself.

She smiles now with an air of timid possibility. Her head slightly tilts towards Henry. Her eyes slant up towards Henry. For a moment she imagines skipping down a yellow brick road with her dear friends and, yes, new business partners. If Dorothy could do it so could she!

Mary is thinking about business--yes, since Rita likes working with mentally ill people and Henry really likes coffee and accounting, what if Mary helps them put their dreams together. Why mentally ill people must need a place to just sit down like ordinary people and have coffee and talk. Maybe everybody just needs a place to feel that they're okay. What did Dorothy keep saying at the end of the movie...there's no place like home, there's no place like home. Maybe the three of them could make a nice homey place for mentally ill people, like she has made for Belinda.

Henry's whole being seems to expand under Mary's attention. She looks at Henry with twinkling significance and simply says, "So you really know about all that stuff?"

Henry nods modestly.

On that next Monday with a supplicating voice piercing the whale songs, Mary offers a suggestion to Rita--carefully. "You know, Rita," her voice softens to a pleading tone, "I wonder--Henry sure is a good person to work with--you know how he likes to go to places and drink coffee--people there, seem real relaxed--well what if we maybe put everything together--you with all your experience with mentally ill people and Henry with the way he likes coffee shops and his accounting stuff--I bet we three could start this place for mentally ill people to come to, like a place where they could feel at home and have coffee?"

Rita's face darkens; that crease between her

eyebrows flickers in response to that challenge. Those eyes shoot sparks at Mary.

Late that afternoon Rita's eyes softly peek out of her bower like the first evening star. "Mary, Mary, I have a wonderful idea. We can do something really visionary and new. I entered this business because I wanted to do something for that mysterious and wonderful man that I met years ago at the library. You remember, Glenn. I want to make the world safer and easier for people like him. Instead of this cold brick building, why don't we set up a real homey place for my dear clients to come to? I'll bet that we can get some sort of funding from the state. Henry can help us with that; he's good at that kind of thing. With my vision and Henry's accounting skills we can pull this off!"

Mary smiles with a not necessarily becoming slyness. At the end of the day she rushes home eager to share her victory with Belinda who is juggling two difficult tasks at the same time. Not only is she painting birds on the stones piled in her kitchen, but in an attempt to assist Mary, she is trying her hand at cooking--rice. Unfortunately the water has all boiled off and the house is filling with smoke.

After turning off the flame, Mary shares her idea. "I have some really swell news."

"Oh no! What's happened now?"

Tripping on Belinda's apprehension, Mary quickly catches her balance and pushes forward. "You know how well the job is going for me, and how nice Rita and Henry are?"

Belinda swallows, panic building in her wild doe eyes.

"Well we three are going to start a company. We really are, and I just know that I have an important part in getting this going. I think maybe we can do it. No matter what happens, they'll be swell to work with. I really want to do this."

"But Mary, you always get us in trouble" And like a great plaid winged condor Belinda sails up the stairs leaving Mary in that room alone.

Chapter 15

"That God damn Mimi won't leave me alone! I talked with Henry about that idea of mine. We'll meet next Wednesday evening at Chow Mien City."

Mary is pleased.

Chow Mien City sits at the base of Fern Ave. Fern Avenue first rises from the heights of the genteel neighborhood of Fernwood; continuing to head downstream, Fern Ave. runs through a nondescript area of apartment buildings and store fronts, picking up debris by the mile. It finally winds its sluggish and no longer pristine way through an area of boarded up houses, abandoned churches, red light flashing saunas, and Chow Mien City.

The oval bar of that Chinese American restaurant is an island spot-lit in gloom, peopled by lonely figures sitting on stools who grasp empty glasses listlessly and stare straight ahead. The bartender moves from figure to figure pointlessly talking. The late spring glare is just beginning to soften by 6 p.m. that fateful Wednesday.

Like the lone representative of some alien race, Henry sits barricaded in his car in the nearly vacant parking lot, waiting. A faint animation sparks his face as he sees Rita's car enter with its single passenger. They are all here.

Rita steps out of the car with taut, commanding steps. Mary slips out more timidly, carrying a paper tablet and a soft smile. Henry simply emerges while no one is looking, "You made it."

Rita nods as she ushers them through the swinging door into the gloom. This is her place. She says a few mysterious hello's to unresponsive figures at the bar, then silently directs her new partners to the darkest corner, perhaps dark enough for stars to shine.

This had been a Mexican restaurant not so long ago. The waitress, uniform still embroidered with tiny sombreros, steps over, "Hi Rita."

"Hi Snickers."

"Do you want the usual?"

Rita smiles with the relief of a kid who has just been invited to play a game. "Sure, Snickers."

As Henry investigates Snickers, body part by body part, he must have noticed the sombreros. "Give me a margarita."

Mary intrigued by the idea of drinking alcohol especially while it was still light, chirps in, "Me too."

The three are alone now, abandoned to the

shadows and Mary's nervous desire to make things work. Henry appears to be stuck in permanent neutral while Rita sputters in rage at Mel. Clearly a more effective and less passionate voice is needed. Mary rises to the occasion. "Henry, Rita and I have been thinking a lot today about this whole new company stuff." Cautious not to identify herself as an independent actor, Mary looks with warm appreciation at Rita. So far, so good. "Rita has all this experience, and I've been assisting her, but neither of us is familiar with accounting. We can even hire people to visit our clients. The Department of Human Services pays for that too."

Rita stirs ominously, as if she had been vaguely accused of something.

Mary back tracks quickly, "Rita really does know a lot about accounting and things like that, but she is going to be very busy."

Rita becomes still.

Henry stirs, roused as if shocked to action. "When I worked for Universal Systems, I supervised the entire accounting department."

Mary nods rapidly, reassuring her too modest partner.

"I went to the library downtown and looked up the legal procedures for starting a business, and I talked to someone at the state. We can get funding for something called a drop-in center. We can also get paid for providing personal care attendants to help our clients at home." He reaches down to a now familiar brief case and picks out forms that he has already begun filling in. He radiates quiet, resourceful strength.

Even in the gloom Mary notices the silky brown hairs on his wrists and just for the briefest of moments she wonders if that hair spreads all the way up his arms across his chest.

Two bright eyes like stars spy Mary's longing glance.

Snickers returns with the drinks: two margaritas and a screw driver. Whether it was the masterful way in which Mary opened the meeting, Henry's surprising ardor, or just the availability of a familiar drink, Rita expands almost filling up that heavy, carved Mexican chair. "Dammit, we can do it! We can set this baby up right under Mel's sneaky gaze. I'll really get him! We can do this business right, my way. I stayed up all last night brain storming trying to think of a name, but Mimi kept bothering me."

Mary could almost see the gates of Oz ahead--somewhere over the rainbow, that's it, The Rainbow. "Boy you sure put in a lot of work Rita. Well maybe, you know, after the storm, comes The Rainbow--do you get it?"

The little cleft between Rita's eyebrows begins to flicker. Brooding she takes another sip of her drink.

"A pot of gold at the other end; sounds good to me." Henry salutes his new partners with his margarita.

"Well, I suppose so; it was my storm after all." Rita concedes not altogether gracefully.

Mary is by now coasting into shadowy contentment. She licks some salt off the rim of her glass. A thin line of a smile curves across her face.

As if animated by some inner explosion, Rita begins jumping up and down on her throne. "We'll do it, Goddamn it! Nobody is going to get in my way this time! I have a mission and nobody is going to fuck with me!" Though her eyes are still shining, words slip away as she appears to lose her bearing.

Mary immediately takes her cue. "Boy, Rita, this is really exciting."

Henry grins.

"Henry, if it's all right with Rita, why don't you maybe go ahead with those forms. Maybe we can even meet next week to kind of keep things moving?" Mary is careful to pose her ideas as questions.

Rita nods after a moment of suspense.

The juke box clicks on and makes a scratching sound before finally slipping into the groove of "Strangers in the Night." Two shadowy figures get up from the bar to dance.

And that's how the business starts, vision warping around private strategies; each new partner attempting to direct the accelerating course with whatever resources they can muster.

The next day Mimi calls Mary at the office, early in the morning, before Rita makes her entrance.

"Hello, The Milk of Human Kindness, Can I help you?"

"Mary, Mary? This is Mimi."

"Oh hi Mimi, how are you this morning?"

"My mommy says that Mel is real bad. Sometimes I get scared. Mommy's so mad at that stinker Mel."

"Mimi, everything is going to be all right with everybody. Your mommy and me and our friend Henry have an idea where everyone is going to live happily ever after over the rainbow like one big family. You too, Mimi."

"Do you think so, Mary? Do you think so?"

"You just wait and see. Everything is going to be more than okay."

"My mommy, too?"

"Especially your mommy."

"Bye, bye, Mary."

"Goodbye, Mimi; take care."

Click.

For some reason unknown to Mary, now that Rita is actually finding her way out of Mel's power, her anger climbs to new heights. Between frequent trips to the copying machine, mining TMHUK's forms and procedures, she keeps muttering, "I'm gonna get that fucker!"

Mary makes a half-hearted attempt to keep the office going while carefully avoiding the "Mel" word. Mary does have misgivings. Fortunately the movie *Thelma and Louise* comes out that summer.

Once every three months Mary throws caution to the wind and treats herself to an afternoon matinee. Opening her hidden bag of popcorn that she brings from home, absorbing the images of the flickering screen, she watches this story of two women, loyal to each other, pushed by conspiring circumstances to become well meaning outlaws. If nothing else, Mary is loyal.

Rita and Mary, secretive as clams, give notice. The new company gathers momentum so easily; it is clearly meant to be. All Rita's explosive energy, all Mary's meek behind the scenes cleverness, all Henry's broad business sense--it all pays off. Each partner secretly takes credit for this miracle. Like clockwork they move closer to the dream which none of them individually is capable of creating.

Mary is becoming a reluctant but budding strategist. After all, she cares about her partners. All she asks in return is simply that everything keeps moving to a happy ending over the rainbow, if not for herself, at least for Mimi. She hopes that someday, she might meet that little dear.

Move along, the company does. The last week at The Milk of Human Kindness goes off without a hitch as The Rainbow edges its way over the horizon. Papers packed, strategies set in motion; the three glide into the future.

Chapter 16

So starts the spinning of The Rainbow, "TRB" to people in the business, fittingly in Rita's abode. They plan to be there for only a few weeks until they find a proper office.

Rita ushers her two collaborators into her house, her little face gleaming in delight as she displays her fake fur sofa and a coffee table covered with a zebra skin on which sits peacock feathers in a brass vase. All these accouterments are set against deep ocher walls. The crevice between her eyebrows flickers as she leads them into the kitchen. Sun shines on a mass of tangled plants working their way over piles of dirty dishes. On the only window sill remaining clear, sits a small pot with screamingly dry soil out of which a feeble plant barely manages to send out two anemic leaves into an unforgiving world.

Coy excitement mounts as Rita introduces them to her bathroom done in sea shell pink. One could imagine this diminutive Venus emerging from that misty bath tub, a playful goddess in her shrine.

Then her face darkens with brooding reverence as they slip into the hall.

"Don't think I'm going to show you my God damned bedroom!"

Rita pauses as if in the midst of some epic struggle. Finally sparkling eyes again peer out of that pert face. She speaks in a diminutive voice. "Well, if you guys really want to, I suppose you can take a teensy look."

Mary still careful to advance no further stretches her large torso around the doorway and catches a glimpse of dusky, jungle green walls and a blood red carpet. She is duly impressed. Henry glances in with casual familiarity and then abandons the two for his computer.

When Rita finally presents Mary with a key to her house, she accepts it with reverence...another step further on that yellow brick road. Henry seems to already have a key.

Mary remembers with tingling embarrassment that she is forgetting the fourth passenger on this trip. After all Dorothy went down that road with three friends. "Rita, where is little Mimi. I was so hoping to meet her?"

Rita's face momentarily disassembles. "Mimi, oh, I sent her off to my mother's. She has the mumps, temporarily of course." The crevice between her eyebrows begins to flicker.

While sitting at his computer Henry casually

says to Mary, "I'll pick you up tomorrow for work. Be ready at 8:00."

8:01, Mary slips out of the door from that dead end house, careful not to wake Belinda. 8:02, over the pounding beat of Henry's new interest, punk rock, Mary's voice can be barely heard, "Hi Henry, how are you doing this morning?"

"Ya."

The need for intimate conversation satisfied, they roar off, Henry driving with the daring of someone who has faced danger without a concern.

Mary has an odd sense that something is mysteriously different; she is beginning to be proud of her deepening intuition. Half way through the trip, Henry abruptly turns the radio off.

Henry speaks. "I had a dream last night."

"Oh Henry, I'd love to hear about it."

"I'm all alone, except there's people all around. Blood starts coming out of my arm. Everyone starts leaving. Blood starts gushing from all different parts of my body. People are running away now. I'm left all alone bleeding."

"Oh Henry. I won't leave you, I promise."

He opens and closes his mouth silently and turns on the radio.

She feels a real warmth for this wounded man. What amazing partners she has. Both have walked into the darkness and come back; they have so much to teach her. She dedicates herself to listening to their stories, and maybe even in some insignificant way, she can help them in their journeys. She brushes aside her own apprehension to focus on their need. She has been preparing for this role her entire life.

This morning that suburban station wagon stops in front of Rita's sleepy home; quietly Henry and Mary step out of the car. After unlocking and opening the front door they wind their way through the kitchen and into the living room where they sit down at the formerly zebra skin clad table to start a day of work. So many people to call, so many things to do, and they still haven't found a permanent home for The Rainbow. The request to set up a drop-in center for mentally ill people sets off an avalanche of paper work from the state. On almost any morning Mary can be seen clutching the phone.

A disembodied voice filters through the fiercely held phone receiver pressed to her ear. "This is the Department of Human Services. We are glad as always to serve you. If you are using a touch tone phone press 1, if not stay om the line." Mary listens to the seamless and reassuring voice.

She carefully follows the orders and presses 1.

This time that voice seems even calmer as if each pressed button draws the caller further into its placid control. "If you would like to receive information about receiving benefits, press 1. If you would like to apply for a job, press 2. If you would like to file a complaint, press 3. For any other reason, press 4."

For some strange reason, Mary always seems driven to press the last mystery button. By now that calm voice is filtering through Mary like an opiate. Drowsily she presses 4.

Now an even calmer voice whispers through the phone. "If you would like to speak to an operator for a list of our personnel, press 1.' If you would like to speak to our operator from the accounting office press 2. If you would like to speak to our central operator press 3. Press 4 for any other reason."

As Mary swirls into numbness, she focuses her faltering awareness on the question she has written on the little pad. She presses 4.

A seductive voice oozes through the receiver. "We at the Department of Human Services deeply appreciate your call. Please wait for the next available operator." The resigned tones of "Let It Be" played by a thousand violins now lilts through the receiver. After about five minutes there is an abrupt click. The music stops, and then after a long, suspenseful moment then teasingly continues.

As Mary is rapidly losing consciousness, a tight, irritated voice intrudes on Mary's repose. "This is Marjorie at the Department of Human Services. What do you want?"

Mary scrambles to collect the bits of her identity. She discovers her name first. "Ahhhh, my name is Mary Blu." Suddenly she remembers something about a rainbow...oh yah. "I, I work for a company called The Rainbow."

Marjorie's breathing is accelerating rapidly, and

there is a clicking sound in the background that is picking up speed.

Suddenly Mary sees the piece of paper leaning against her phone. "Well, you see Marjorie, I have a question. I keep listening for the right buttons to press, but nothing seems to fit. I sure hope this is the right one and you can help me."

Marjorie's breathing is not only increasing in speed but also seems to be getting louder. The clicking sound increases rapidly. "I don't have all day. There are people waiting who actually have questions."

Concern for Marjorie and her busy schedule radiates through Mary's body. "Oh I'm so sorry. It sounds like you really have a real hard job. Some days are just like that. I just have this little question. I won't take long. It's just a little question, and then I'll be all set. Is that all right, Marjorie? I really appreciate your time, you being so busy and all."

Some natural disaster seems to be occurring on the other end of the line.

Mary prevails over the tumult. "I've got this form here that I'm filling out. We want to start a drop-in center and a home visiting service..."

Marjorie barges in. If this is a question about one of our forms, you need to speak to some one in our forms department. Please hold on....." There are several minutes of silence followed by a click. Then a familiar sound buzzes through the receiver until another and more authoritative voice replaces it. "If you'd like to make a call, please hang up and try again."

Before Mary has a chance to try again, the phone rings.

"The Rainbow, this is Mary Blu, can I help you?"

"Mary, this is Mona, is Henry there?"

"No, ah, I bet he's out to get some coffee, but he'll be back soon I think, Mona."

"Is he all right, Mary? Is my Henry all right?"

"Sure Mona, he's doing real well."

"Are you sure, are you really sure. I worry about him sometimes spending all those extra hours at the office, especially on weekends. I hardly get to see him anymore."

"That sounds hard."

"My Henry is so sensitive. He gets so easily upset. As a therapist, I know about these things. He had a troubled childhood. His father yelled and screamed around the house all the time. His mother was a real martyr, bless her soul. Henry was the only one his father didn't scream at...such a good boy. Of course there was that little time he got in trouble. When he was about sixteen..."

Mary is more interested in people who are troubled, not people getting into trouble. "Well gee, Mona thanks for telling me all this stuff. I'll let Henry know that you called. I'm sure he'll be pleased."

By the time Henry gets back, a customary commotion finishes in the bathroom; Rita reveals herself to her attending partners, eyes sparkling under those little bangs.

Mary is relieved that she hasn't been brainstorming. Sometimes the storms are so powerful that they prevent Rita's emergence for days at a time. In fact both Mary's partners have a way of disappearing.

In her large hands Rita holds a hairy, gray object about six inches long that fortunately isn't moving, at least for Mary's sake.

"I found it in the yard you guys, a squirrel tail, all cut off and waiting to be picked up."

Henry glances up and then returns to more interesting, inanimate information on his computer.

Mary squeamish about anything that is cut off, smiles tightly. She is able to manage, "I suppose so."

Rita grasps the hairy rodent tail, winding it between her fingers. She freezes for a moment as if caught in neutral. As the crevice between her eyebrows begins flickering, she pushes her treasure within six inches of Mary's face. "God damn it Mary, look at it!"

"It's icky."

Rita stares at Mary and then rushes out of the room.

Twenty minutes later a distant and composed Rita reenters the scene. "I was goddamn brainstorming all night. I know what we have to do to get this baby off the ground. What we need is a brochure!"

Mary nods reassuringly.

Henry continues to punch keys.

"Don't you see? It's what we fucking need. I

want you both to stop everything right now! We'll all brainstorm and finish this puppy even if we have to work twenty four hours a day!"

"Click, click, click," Henry, stranger to the cosmos, continues to press keys on the computer keyboard.

Mary panicking at the idea of being locked up for twenty four hours with Rita, finally says, "Rita, what a swell idea, but I have to make these urgent calls today."

There is a moment of silence absolute as ever known. Starting from that tiny blinking spot between her eyebrows, Rita's face begins disorganizing feature by feature. From out of that chaos, a screaming voice issues. "How dare you question my judgment?! We fucking need this pamphlet now! Now! You hear me, assholes, now!"

Mary fades in and out of this once routine day. She hears a single bird call outside the window and follows it out there with her mind for just a moment. Perhaps it is from the perspective of the bird that a moment of clarity seeps through her consciousness. "Rita, please don't scream at me."

The disorganized fragments of Rita's face explode across the room in a blast. "Get out! Get out of here you bitch, goddamn it! Right now! Now!"

Up to this point Henry has been obliviously working on the computer. The blast must have triggered some automatic defense mechanism; he casually gets up as if he has just completed a rather satisfying day and begins walking out of the house.

Unwilling to expose her rear, Mary backs out. Screams shake the house.

Silently Henry and Mary slip into the car reversing this morning's sequence. Henry genially reaches to turn on the radio, but is briefly interrupted by Mary's pleading voice.

"Did you see what she did?"

Henry turns his placid face toward her. "That's just Rita." He casually turns on the radio.

As the broken strains of punk rock fill the station wagon, Mary feels, well, reassured. Henry is so fair not to take sides. He's steely calm under fire and a good man to have around. For Mary the day ends in guarded optimism.

The next morning Henry and Mary follow their usual sequence, but a surprise awaits optimistic Mary. As usual she starts her day by reaching for her scheduling book. Only this time, she doesn't have to page through it to find her place...the hairy chord of a squirrel's tail marks the spot.

All Mary can think of is that scene in *Whatever Happened to Baby Jane?* when deranged Bette Davis put a dead bird instead of an omelet on paralyzed Joan Crawford's breakfast tray. "Henry, look what's lying in my scheduling book. It's horrible."

Henry glances up from his computer and then quickly and silently returns his attention to those undemanding keys.

Mary doesn't hear the gleeful little giggle from the dark bedroom sanctuary.

After an absence of three days, Rita returns to her routine and once again swirls into the living room. She is in a luminous, sympathetic phase. "Oh Mary, how are you today?"

"Fine Rita good to see you," but Mary keeps her eyes down.

"Henry, what a delight to see you!"

With a fleeting hint of a smile he shrugs his shoulders.

That afternoon while Mary is microwaving a hot dog until it splits open and becomes like curled cardboard, Rita breezes in.

"Oh, Mary."

"Hi Rita."

"Did I ever show you this?" She motions sweetly to that struggling little plant perched on the window sill. Eyes brimming she explains, "This plant was given to me by a woman who used to be my dear and trusted friend. She betrayed me but I still have her sweet little plant. She pinched a leaf off and ground it maliciously between her fingers. Mary I'm so glad we're friends. You mean so much to me!"

Mary nods.

Chapter 17

Next morning, enveloped in her over-sized bed, Rita's haven is once again troubled by the muffled sounds of footsteps outside her bedroom door, clicking of computer keys, and Mary's beseeching voice pleading on the phone.

Rita's own voice cries out to be heard. She grabs her notebook and pen from the table next to her bed.

Rita's diary: October 5, 1995 "My God! What can I do? I'm trapped. Those two out there, I know they're talking about me. I've worked so hard to scratch my way back from the edge of darkness. Mary is so smug with that soft, knowing smile of hers, as if she could actually understand all that I've experienced. This business is my life. At first she seemed like the perfect helpmate, thoughtful and caring. Then very, very slowly and slyly she has begun extending her control, first just a little reassuring nod or subtle grimace. I WON'T FUCKING HAVE IT, SHE'S NOSING

IN ON MY BUSINESS. Those two come together and go off together leaving me all alone here to figure things out. When I struggle all night with an idea and try to explain it in the morning Mary looks at me like I'm spoiled meat. If she didn't have her goddamn head stuck in her cunt, she'd see that I'm the one around here who keeps everything together. I've been doing this business longer than anyone else. How dare she think that she knows better? And Henry, I'm so disappointed in him submitting to her seduction. He sniffs her butt and follows that bitch when he should go along with me, me. He is even starting to smile at her.

`Yes, little Rita, I know what's best for you. This isn't going to hurt, I'll take care of you. There, little Rita, what a good little girl.' They treat me like I'm crazy. Now I can't leave this room without either of them looking at me wondering, 'Is she better now, will she be quiet like a good girl?' I won't be fucking quiet. This is my house...my goddamn business. How dare they do this to me in my fucking home? I CAN'T GET AWAY! Oh my God! What am I going to do! I stay in this room all day and night and I just keep spinning. I hate them! My body shakes. My fists are like balls of steel. Even when I turn on my videos I see Mary and Henry on the screen smiling at each other. I try to read but start wondering what deep, bad part of me makes Henry leave me for that bitch. I'm afraid. I'm so alone. What if things fall apart again and I have to go back to that horrible darkness? Nobody believes me. They smile and want me to keep quiet. 'My Rita, don't make a fuss now.' No matter how restricted my diet gets, my life is going out of focus. Last night I binged on a whole pint of frozen yogurt. I even had to send Mimi away for a while. Who'll take care of Mimi? God damn Mimi won't ever leave me alone. I can't stand being alone. Where's Mimi?"

Chapter 18

The three partners have been at Rita's place for three weeks. They are sitting down together around the Zebra skinned table to explore office rental ads with a sense of urgency. Mary haltingly reads each ad, while an excited Rita pastes little gold stars on any ad that shows promise. Henry is involved in an even more arduous task, metamorphosis. Somewhere between the bright centrally located office space with 1,000 square feet and the large over-sized studio that could double as an office, Henry announces, "My name is now Hernando."

Mary looks reassuringly at Hernando and continues reading ads. With her newly discovered perceptivity she has her own silent theory: it is all those margaritas he's been drinking.

By this time Rita is jumping up and down, her large fists scattering stars across the table, "That's it, that's it Mary, read it again."

Mary pulls herself from the silent web of her theories about Hernando and bobs her head as she attempts to understand what she is reading. "Lovely carriage house in picturesque Fernwood perfect for residence or office space. Children, cats, dogs, disturbing relatives welcome, ask for Ariadne."

Rita is now covered in stars. "This is a message meant just for us. I know about these things. Suddenly she frowns as if interrupted by some mysterious force. "What in the fuck is this shit about Hernando?"

Hernando stops pecking at the computer keys, looking up with uncharacteristic animation. You never heard of "Hernando's Hide Away?"

Rita looks puzzled.

Hernando slyly smiles at her and starts softly singing off tune.

"I know a dark secluded place,
Where no one knows your face,
A glasses of wine, a fast embrace,
It's called Hernando's hide away"

Then once again he turns back to his computer as if nothing had ever happened.

Chapter 19

$\mathcal{A}$riadne and Fernwood enter the lives of Rita, Hernando and Mary Blu.

Once upon a time, Ariadne Bailey had been a beauty queen, or at least runner up for some contest in Tennessee. Certain impassioned suitors even called her a goddess. Indeed her mother, a doyenne of a high toned local drama club in Chattanooga, named her daughter after her starring role in *Ariadne: a Greek Tragedy*.

Ariadne grew up to have chestnut hair of legendary length, features fine, carved out of butter, a ship launching smile, and legs too good for walking. Perhaps even then dread was peeking in her mirror. Fortunately or not, she was too distracted by the attentions of her gentleman callers to notice.

She studied to be an elementary teacher knowing full well that some handsome, debonair, rich man would relieve her of her burdens and take her as a milky treasure. He did. Unfortunately after having born a child and having spent too many years cosseted away in that suburban home, she lost her blush; her husband decided that he never really did love her anyway. As in many of these stories, he found a younger woman to sympathize with him and not bear his children. She was smarter than that, having never been a beauty queen.

Ariadne found herself aging, her still long chestnut hair streaked with strands of crispy gray. Her son, her responsibility, wanted to be just like dad. What to do? The next years seemed frozen in complaining discontent for Ariadne.

Then one particularly cold night in January she woke; some fire inside was being madly stoked. In the next few days she realized that she was being plagued by some sort of unpredictable internal combustion. An electric fan became her nightly companion. Even her body was now beyond control.

Some force of nature within had begun transforming her life. That next morning, driving to work, and she had to work now, she found herself weeping for each squirrel that she saw, smashed on the road. Then she understood...menopause: the dreaded menopause, the end of maidenly hopes for happy endings.

She began, perhaps for the first time in her life, to reflect. What happened to her? The princess? The wife? The abandoned woman? She stopped the car and stared at the face in the rear view mirror. She studied that mask: the pucker lines around its lips sucking up red lipstick, the hair around the mask, crispy and wild. Then a strange thing happened, faster than an instant, for the first time she understood, no, not understood...realized that the image in the mirror wasn't her. That image in her eyes and anyone else's eyes, wasn't her. She was here, here, here. To no one in particular she whispered, "Isn't this strange?" and then smiled a secret smile. That look of betrayal that had been pinching up her face these last months, smoothed out. She wasn't even angry that her son had left to live with his father.

The firestorm of menopause was steadying to a summer glow and without even trying, the bushel had been lifted, and the light within began to shine.

Now she could make choices, mistakes and all. This second time she married well, one of the Ferns of Fernwood...Roy. The first Fern did not come over on the Mayflower. In fact Isaak Fernansky was spilled out on Ellis Island with hundreds of thousands of other refugees who lost their names and their histories during the last century.

With desperation and no past, Isaac Fern rode that oblivious wave of people that overwhelmed The Great Plains driving out and murdering the longtime residents (an old yellow tin type of Isaac proudly standing on a mountain of buffalo carcasses used to hang proudly in Fernhall until Ariadne took up residence there). Isaac became a farmer, then invested in railroads and eventually founded a dynasty built on soybeans.

Without a past, and the future already surmounted, Isaac married a Scandinavian girl, and in the next three generations their homogenized progeny made their gradual descent down through their progenitor's soy bean fortune into threadbare gentility. Roy, the last of the Ferns, married late in life. He loved gardening and Ariadne. Their childless marriage was the final chapter of the waning Fern Family Saga.

Thanks to Roy's inherited farming skills there was a cellar of newly canned tomatoes, string beans, apple sauce, and pickles; but property taxes and the heating bills were eating up the last of the Fern Fortune.

Pondering the vicissitudes of life, Ariadne looks out over the carefully trimmed yards and grand houses of the other denizens of Fernwood, over the Fernwood Country Club and across an invisible barrier to lower Fernwood and Thorndike Towers mounting ominously in the distance. Thorndike Towers is public housing.

Perhaps it was her sixty five years, but she knew that none of us stay here permanently. Her gaze was pricked by the point of a weather vane surmounting the peak of her unused carriage house--unused carriage house. Ariadne had learned to consider options. That's it! The Ferns hadn't had carriages for years and Roy usually parked his old Ford near the apple tree. Not only could she solve their cash flow dilemma, but she could also get a chance to add a little color to the neighborhood.

Chapter 20

The wind rushes through the old trees lining Fern Avenue, tearing off yellow leaves and driving them swirling down the block. Two cars stop outside of a turreted three story home on Fernwood Avenue. Rita bursts out of the driver's side of the Volvo; she is on a mission. Hernando slips out of his decaying station wagon as silently as a thief. Finally Mary cautiously opens her door and lumbers out clutching an open newspaper. The determined wind flaps the paper like gull wings sending Mary at an unaccustomed speed after her companions. The more she tries to gain control, the faster the wind impels her toward her future.

Rita is already through the front door; Hernando slipping in right after. Mary running, driven by the wind, takes up the rear several steps behind.

Inside that mansion something like a cocktail party is taking place. The guests are various but each clasps a little want ad which seems to serve as a ticket for admission. A round woman with pigeons perched on her tie dyed shoulders casually is sipping something from a martini glass. Another woman is sitting on the floor playing with four children each a different shade of color. Two young men are holding hands try to explain to Ariadne the importance of calling themselves queer. Roy is serving tomatoes and green beans.

The door swings open violently and white winged Mary is shoved in by a last gust of wind. All eyes turn to the tumbling Mary. Her feet can't keep pace with her forward moving torso. In the center of the room she collides with a very large St. Bernard and after wobbling finally lands on her back, the newspaper covering her head and body. Her legs sticking out of the newspaper still scramble around in a futile attempt to maintain her lost balance. Then all motion stops as this large lump of a woman surrenders to her newspaper shroud.

Ariadne watches the inert body under the newspaper. Smiling graciously at her guests she glides over and kneels next to the newspaper covered form. Ever so gently she tips up a corner of the paper and peers underneath to see Mary's face, her eyes squeezed close. "What a pleasant surprise my dear!"

Mary opens one eyelid.

Ariadne smiles.

Mary closes that one lid and sheepishly both her eyes open.

Ariadne catches Mary's fleeing attention. "I love surprises and you are the biggest surprise today."

Mary manages a sheepish smile and takes a deep determined breath. "I came with Rita and Hen...I mean Hernando...that's his new name. We started this company...I know it's not much and you look like a very busy person and all, but I was wondering if by any chance we could rent your garage house for a place that mentally ill people could come to and relax like it's a home. We'd call it the Rainbow...just because rainbows are kind of hopeful, you know, well and they're so pretty...you don't have to or anything, I just thought I'd ask."

Rita jumps in. "My name is Rita Reinke and it's my idea. I have a mission."

Hernando sidles up to Rita. "My name is Hernando. I take care of the money."

Ariadne turns toward the pair studying them for an instant. She turns back Mary. "So you and your fine friends intend to set up a business here for mentally ill people."

Mary closes her eyes again for instant, takes a deep breath and opens them. "We really do. I don't think I've ever really wanted to do anything before... probably...I think." She fixes hopeful eyes on Ariadne.

Ariadne slowly looks around the room at all the hopeful people. Was that a hint of sadness in her eyes? Once again she rests her eyes on Mary. "I do so like surprises, and rainbows; they're one of my favorite things." She looks over at Roy. "We have found our new tenant."

Chapter 21

The Rainbow had been set in motion years earlier. Back then several politicians began thinking that they didn't like the idea of institutions for mentally ill people. Since it was only the idea that they didn't like, it was very easy for them to simply decide to stop it. It's so easy with ideas after all. Once an idea is stated and put on paper, the problem is solved.

In the spring following, that idea was formalized and sent out as an email throughout the state. Now former residents of those institutions began popping up like tender tulips all over the inner city. They sprung up in pathways already worn down by discontent and violence. They huddled at curb sides afraid of the next idea from someone who didn't know them.

The Rainbow, like an unsuspected cottonwood seed, one night floated in that bureaucratic chaos, landed, and before any bureaucrat could eliminate it, landed and sprouted and began growing.

For Mary the Land of Oz is becoming flesh, materializing moment by moment. Hernando, who takes care of the company credit card begins purchasing chairs, sofas, desks and a large computer that he assures his partners is capable of doing anything. Each night Rita struggles to birth new plans and games. Dreams of new recipes for forbidden treats dance in her head. Best of all she stocks up on stars. Mary fills out more smudged forms and makes so many calls to The Department of Human Services that they grudgingly begin rooting for her and The Rainbow.

The day after Christmas the three pile boxes of papers, three desks, assorted furniture, and a new deluxe state of the art computer into a rented truck and drive to Fernwood. Up the driveway, past the great house, and there, like some belated present stands the carriage house, but instead of a bow, Ariadne and Roy have painted a rainbow that starts from ground, arching over the doorway all the way up to the roof and back again.

As they step over the threshold, the two phones begin ringing simultaneously; social workers are calling to find out if their clients can begin coming to The Rainbow.

The business is open, and this very day at 12:00 noon Rita and Mary head out to intake clients, Mary leaving a "see you later Hernando" hanging in the air. The two pile into Rita's large Volvo to spread the word. Rita places her big hands on the steering wheel and stares out. Stillness fills the car. Her face looks quiet and intent...she is starting her mission.

"Mary, who are we scheduled to see today?"

Without a wobbling head or apology Mary looks at the papers she is holding. "Um, we have this new client downtown...according to the social worker, he's paranoid schizophrenic and lives alone and doesn't leave the house for days at a time...leaves all the blinds down. At night, neighbors complain about the screaming noises."

"That doesn't sound too bad, pretty straight forward. Is he suicidal?" Rita holds steady.

Mary envelopes herself in her errand of mercy and something almost like confidence steadies her voice. "The social worker doesn't mention it; there is something about being threatened with eviction... the noise at night and something about a smell too."

"What's the other intake?"

"It's down in Thorndike Hall, a client just out of the hospital...again. Some vague personality disorder...frequent suicide attempts, anxiety and panic. Social worker doesn't specify a diagnosis."

Rita's face transforms into desperate anger. "Watch out when they don't fucking specify!"

"Um, why don't you take a right at this corner, Rita? I think it's maybe that brick building."

The car stops. Rita grabs her purse and lunges out of the door towards the entrance of the building. Mary takes a deep breath, picks up the briefcase and hesitantly steps out of the car. Rita presses the apartment buzzer, presses again--nothing happens, presses again and the security lock reluctantly clicks open. It is a new building, but already cigarette burns and grease spots mark the gray carpet. The florescent lights hum, periodically strobing on and off. As the two look up to the second floor landing they see a very large man standing sentinel. His pant legs barely reach the tops of his ankles, and a rope tied around his waist attempts to bring together the divided shores of his pants, leaving a "V" of stained underwear showing. The strained buttons over his round stomach open to hairy skin.

When the duo get within eight steps of him he turns away and walks mechanically to his door, leaving it open a few inches. The partners perch there. Mary quietly taps the door. Rita talking very formally. "Charles, I'm from The Rainbow."

Mary waits for few beats, then, "Hi Charles, my name is Mary. Um, can we talk with you for a few minutes?"

The silence stretches out. Finally, suspiciously Charles answers, "Just shut the door behind you."

The room is piled high with newspapers, graying clothes, and a large heap of tin cans. The kitchen overflows with dirty dishes, spoiled food, and cereal boxes. A large coffee pot perks amidst the chaos.

Cigarette butts reside on little burnt islands, marking the carpet.

Charles stares at them like an unrelenting stone.

Rita and Mary move very slowly.

Mary smiles. "Boy, this is really a nice, big apartment. Do you recycle cans? My sister Belinda is always talking about wanting to do that."

Charles nods and just for a second looks at Mary with curiosity.

Rita sits there strangely vacant

He glances apologetically at the window sealed off with blinds. "It's a mess, a real mess, this place is a mess. Do you want some coffee?" He starts toward the kitchen, then stops, hesitant or even frightened to pass in front of his guests. He bolts by them, then stops, staring at them fiercely. "Who sent you? What do you want? You better not try to make me go to the hospital!"

Rita and Mary don't make eye contact with Charles or each other.

Charles suddenly deflates, his face dropping into his hands.

In the softest of voices Mary says, "Sorry it's so hard...I mean..." and just leaves those words gently in front of him.

Rita snaps out of her fugue state and once again is an adult on a mission. "Charles we may be able to give you a hand with things, and we won't make you go to the hospital. We have this place were you can come where no one will think you're strange." Then she loses her train of thought.

Mary takes over again. "The thing is, you won't have to come...nobody will force you, but it's a nice place with coffee and treats and maybe fun. Sometimes we can even send out people to come in and help with things like grocery shopping or cooking…only if you want to."

Charles puzzles over the situation. "Do you two want some coffee?"

"Sure Charles," they say simultaneously, and for the briefest moment the two partners exchange a moment of understanding.

"You can call me Charlie."

In the next hour, with starts and stops, twenty pages of state mandated forms that involve intrusive questions are filled out--a dance the three performed to a subtle hesitant rhythm.

Then some inner clock reminds Mary that it is time to end. "Charlie, thanks for all your help."

Rita's earrings jangle, angry at the interruption, then relieved. She catches her balance.

Mary asks, "If you come and visit us, is there any special treat you'd like?"

Charlie twists his hands together. "My mom used to make rice crispy bars, with lots of butter." And then he looks down as if he had just violated some sacred trust.

Mary watches him. "Wow, you like rice crispy bars too, Charlie! Sometimes my sister Belinda and I can eat a whole pan of them."

Charlie laughs, easy, as if his guests had just passed another test.

Rita and Mary get up. Rita once more in the lead. He follows walking them to the landing where again he turns into a stony sentinel, protecting himself from unknowable forces.

Rita plunges back into the car; Mary slides in carefully.

"Boy, Rita, it was a little tense there for a moment. Rita, um, this next one's at Thorndike Towers."

Rita's hands tighten on the wheel as she stares out as rain splashes the windshield and slithers down the glass. Her hand clicks the windshield wipers on, adding a swishing beat to the steady beat of rain.

The next client, Priscilla Emerson, lives in The Towers. This residence is often the first destination for people fresh out of the hospital. The twin towers morosely loom over the lower end of Fern Avenue. Mary presses Priscilla's buzzer at the building entrance and introduces herself. A voice crackles out of the little metal box and like magic the door swings open. They enter. The gray industrial carpet in the lobby has long since been replaced by hard tiles that won't soak up disturbing liquids. Noise echoes up the towers' hollow core in a broken melody of whispers and screams.

They step into the elevator. Mary gingerly presses a button labeled "UP." The doors slide open--they enter--they doors seal them inside its belly. Complaining, it jerks them up to the fifteenth floor.

The elevator releases them. Their footsteps toll against the dingy green tiles. A small, pale blue wreathe hangs on Priscilla's door. As Mary is about to gently pat on the door, it swings open revealing a woman in her thirties, loose, long hair swirling around eyes that burn with apprehension. "Are you from The Rainbow?"

"Yes, my name is Mary."

Rita studies Priscilla's face, then turns away abruptly. She freezes in place.

Priscilla's voice filters through her trembling body. "I'm glad to meet you." She offers a thin hand to her guests.

Mary glances at Rita for a second, and then with her new found resourcefulness takes charge. "My name is Mary…good to meet you."

Priscilla's voice steels as she responds to the intruders. "Please come in and sit down. My therapist said that you might be able to help me."

Mary jumps in, "I sure hope so Priscilla."

Priscilla nods faintly signaling the process to begin. Mary continues to take the lead, "Unfortunately Rita and I have this bunch of papers to fill out…we'll need to ask you questions about yourself."

Priscilla face seems to shatter.

Rita clenches her fists and once again finds her focus. "I know it's hard to have strangers come in and ask for personal information. People asking all kinds of questions as if they want to pin you down and smash you into little pieces."

Priscilla makes eye contact with Rita. "It's just so difficult. I go into the hospital so much. When I'm in there, I can't stand it; but when I'm home and alone, I'm frightened. I go to therapy and I read whatever I can to help myself. My psychiatrist keeps trying new medications, but nothing works; I just get worse. I want to scream and disappear." Priscilla starts to cry, not dramatic tears, but the kind that seep out pressured by unrelenting despair.

Rita now listens in some kind trance.

Oblivious to her own tears Priscilla continues, "Sometimes I feel like everybody knows about me and talks about my problems as if I'm not real, but just part of their jobs. Each year I fill out hundreds of papers trying to describe myself, and I don't know all the people that read them. Bits of me are torn away every time. But I need help, I need help so badly." Priscilla starts rocking.

Mary nods slowly, not the wobbly nodding of false reassurance, but with a slow steady rhythm.

Priscilla takes charge again. "Sometimes it would help me if I had a place to go where someone wasn't trying to find something wrong with me. When you're mentally ill people are always examining you, looking for signs that they're not like you. Sometimes I can't leave the apartment at all and it would help me if someone came in once and a while to help me to the grocery store or just reminded me to brush my hair. Sometimes I'm so frightened I can't move, and when someone comes by I can get out of it a little."

Then the three do the paperwork dance. But even dancing carefully, more privacy is torn away from Priscilla, each dancer hoping that something good will come of it. Finally it is over.

Priscilla's face a battlefield of grief and gratitude says, "Thank you for coming."

No longer capable of offering a hand, Priscilla escorts them to the door leaving a quavering goodbye echoing in the hallway.

Mary and Rita return to the car. Once in that still, closed off place, Rita looks at Mary, "Goddamn it Mary! I recognize her. She lived at TMOHK...she was also in the hospital when I was there. She looked like she was getting better. Why does it have to be that way? You struggle like you're drowning and get so scared you can't even comb your own fucking hair! The only thing you can do is get worse." Rita stares at Mary with fierce accusing eyes.

Chapter 22

Clients are beginning to stream under The Rainbow...one minor detail. The Rainbow which takes care of mentally ill people is funded by The Mental Health Department which is part of the Department of Human Services. To people in the business, MI (mentally ill) clients are funded by MHD (Minnesota Health Department) which is part of DHS (Department of Human Services).

This very day right before lunch, the governor, an accountant, is looking at the budgets of various state departments, nipping and tucking. He spies unruly financial figures from something called MHD which is part of DHS. MHD looks like an unnecessarily expensive proposition. After asking his assistant what those three miscreant letters mean, the governor takes a red ball point pen, circles the increasing numbers and wrote, "Cut this" in tight, regular letters.

This message rolls down to DHS, concern and

disapproval snowballing. Fortunately DHS can let this blame accumulating problem pass down to MHD. The further it passes down the bureaucracy of MHD, the more mass and momentum build up. The amount of work to implement pronouncements expands in reverse proportion to the amount of power a bureaucrat possesses. What had been a rather casual jaunt for the governor becomes a nightmare for the lower rung bureaucrats whose futures now hinge on an immediate solution. Someone is surely to blame. Fortunately for them, they can pass the buck on to the lowest rung of all, the people who are being served.

Hernando picks up Mary as usual the next morning. Car safely docked under The Rainbow, Mary steps out and winds her way up the sidewalk before she notices that Hernando appears unable to successfully complete his exit from the car. Someone is in need. Urgency impels her back to the car. Hernando is using both of his hands to transfer his left leg onto the street. That's when Mary notices a cloth bandage winding around his calf. His pant leg is split up to his thigh to accommodate the unusually large width.

"Hernando, what happened?"

He turns his drooping face to Mary, gently opening and closing his mouth.

"Here let me help you, I'm a nurse after all." Four hands free up his leg.

As if to reward her for her help, Hernando speaks. "The bugger bit me."

"Who bit you Hernando?"

"The bugger just ate my leg."

"Your leg?" Mary was trained in the subtle nursing technique of repeating the last word of someone's response in order to encourage them to comment further.

Hernando lays his moist hand on Mary's shoulder to steady himself. "I was cutting down some brush around the house. I looked up. I looked down and the chain saw was biting into my leg, like it was hungry. The bugger was eating my leg! It didn't even hurt."

Mary gives profuse reassurances and wobbly physical support.

About two hours later, Rita enters under The Rainbow and into their lives. "Did you see this fucking DHS bulletin? They're trying to put us out of business!"

Mary, guarding herself from Rita's eruptions, listens noncommittally, but sympathetically of course.

"Do you hear me? They're trying the fuck to put us out of business!"

Mary rouses, "Oh Rita, that sounds pretty bad, why maybe don't you let me look at it?"

Rita reluctantly relinquishes the paper, throwing it on the table. "Take a look at that!"

Hernando sits, mechanically tapping on computer keys.

As Rita grabs a chair and slams it down, she knocks against Hernando's leg. "What in the hell happened to you?"

He looks up from his steady task, "This weekend

it happened…a chain saw." He disappears back into his computer.

Mary silently picks up the offending bulletin, reading it with even more care than her monthly gas bill.

Rita stares at her accusingly, "Well, what in the fuck are we going to do Miss Smarty Pants?"

Mary ponders the information, exercising her burgeoning shrewdness, "You know, I bet we could call up DHS and just talk to them and say how what we do is really important."

"Swell, as if there's anybody who gives a rat's damn."

Even to Mary, her advice seems flimsy, but since nobody else has anything to offer she decides to call DHS tomorrow morning, early.

After a nice little chat with Jane, the operator, Mary reaches a person named Annette, a very apologetic person with a small voice whose job it is to explain dire news to panicking mental health providers, MHP's to people in the business. Annette who is new to the job perhaps recognizes a kindred soul in Mary. A meeting is set up. Much to Mary's surprise, DHS and an MHP will meet with The Rainbow. Mary is proud of herself; not that she can let anybody know.

Chapter 23

R ita's diary: January 22, 1995...I had a dream last night and woke up screaming. I was standing in front of a judge. It wasn't an actual courtroom, but a kind of back office. The judge, a soft plump person, no wrinkles or worries, like a Pillsbury dough boy, sits behind a towering desk that dwarfs me. This judge is sentencing me to confinement at a state hospital for the mentally ill. Behind me is a friend; I feel tender support and concern coming from that direction. In spite of the terrible situation, I feel that somebody knows what I'm going through and respects me. I tell the judge, "You've never really lived, always trying to make things safe. You destroy people who take chances."

My words drop unheard as I am sentenced. I turn around to look at the face of my friend, but only see the face of the magistrate behind me. I look back and forth. They're the same god damn person! My ears are ringing now and I'm screaming. Just before the dream shatters, I think of Mary and her shenanigans.

Goddamn Mimi won't leave me alone. Just when I'm doing all right, she keeps coming out and bothering me. Doesn't she know mommy has to make her living?

Chapter 24

In spite of the fact that she knows this meeting won't be worth a rat's ass, the morning of this unpromising occasion, Rita shaves her legs, does her nails, and picks out a flowing black power dress to wear. Mary spends her morning on the treadmill of increasing paper work triggered by the tightly written red script of the governor. Hernando almost forgets about the event; fortunately Mona calls to remind him.

The morning of the meeting Mary keeps anxiously reminding her two partners about the meeting. As soon as she lurches towards the door in hopes of triggering an exodus, Rita has to check her hair or touch up her nails one last time. There is always something Hernando has to do before they leave. Finally all three pile into Rita's car, ten minutes late already.

As minutes tick off on the freeway, Mary's stomach

is sinking. By the time Rita takes a wrong exit adding another ten minutes to their road time, Mary begins tumbling into panic. Finally twenty five minutes late, they land at the huge monolith tower of DHS; Mary scurrying to speed things up, Rita moving with the stateliness of Cleopatra, and Hernando with a little smile on his face.

They walk into the conference room. Annette is now regretting that she invited her boss, an important upper, middle level bureaucrat. In spite of Mary's explanation about car trouble, things are off to an unfortunate start.

Annette opens the meeting. "We at DHS are always pleased to talk with MHC's such as you folks from The Rainbow. We at DHS are very concerned about all our MI clients." She then describes how things really won't be different except for much more paperwork which should make delivery of services less expensive. Services to MI clients will be streamlined. Annette's boss keeps glancing between her watch and the three middle aged characters opposite her. Hernando is staring intensely at something above her head. Rita keeps shaking those strange dangling metal earrings that look almost like bullets. Mary squirms desperately against the too tight confines of her white uniform, wondering if this really was such a good idea after all.

Annette meekly winds down to silence; clearly it is time for somebody from TR to address DHS. Unfortunately Hernando is busy staring out in space.

Rita is preoccupied with her own heavy breathing. Mary, who is always eager to fill up any void, speaks up with fitting deference. "Annette," suddenly Mary forgets her line of thought, wondering if she ever had one. With a reassuring flash she remembers that she can always start any statement with a compliment. "I...um, really appreciate your inviting us here. It's so nice that you care about our little company, but, but it's even more wonderful that you care about those people that need us." The broken pace of her speech makes her sound choked up. "Now, I would just like to see if I've understood you all right. We will be able to continue with helping people, but we'll just have to do a whole bunch more paper work that I'm sure will save a lot of money. Services will only be cut just a little." She pauses breathless as if she has just triumphantly climbed a mountain.

A violent jangling sound breaks out next to Mary. Rita's black form swirls up with the righteousness of an angry prophetess. For a brief moment she even captures Hernando's attention. "You're trying to destroy this company! How can you do this to me, me! I won't stand for it. I know important people, and we'll use those goddamn big guns if you try to get rid of us. You just wait and see!"

The upper, middle level bureaucrat wonders if those bullet earrings can actually be used. Annette flinches imperceptibly, wondering if Rita actually has big guns up those loose sleeves.

In a desperate effort to salvage the meeting,

something stir in Mary's stomach even deeper down than all her embarrassment, a cottonwood seed perhaps. She remembers that crumbled handwritten list of all the things that she needed to complete that day. The room is very quiet and she feels the slightest tremor of possibility. Without even thinking she sticks her hand in her pocket and slowly opens the crumbling paper. She starts to read about Charlie and Priscilla and all the other people who have started coming into the Rainbow. In the silence her hesitancy voice poignantly rings. The various bureaucrats start nodding their heads sympathetically. With modest delight Mary realizes that for these few moment, people are listening.

The top med level bureaucrat jots down something on a piece of paper. He looks up, his eyes are strangely damp. "Thanks for breaking this down for us. I will consider your recommendations." The other bureaucrats nod in agreement.

The room is once again filled with rustling murmurs. Mary's moment has passed and she knows, knows that something good has happened. She knows she needs to mark the spot. Her faltering voice seeps through the commotion. "I feel...happy...that you have listened."

People start getting up, the meeting clearly a success. Rita, Hernando, and Mary file out. As Rita plows through the brightly lit maze of halls, she turns around to her partners. "I fucking showed them. They can't do that to us!"

"Ya, we sure did okay today, "Mary joins in."

Rita focuses her stormy eyes on Mary.

Quickly Mary appends her response. "You were really dynamic Rita."

Momentarily satisfied, Rita turns around continuing her course. "I'm sure as hell not going to do any of that extra paper work!" Rita decides not to go to work for a few days.

Chapter 25

Mary's desk piles high with forms, but The Rainbow continues to shine. Five days a week the door stands open in invitation. Mary and Hernando arrive at 9 a.m., unlocking the door under the rainbow to begin another day. Mary washes out the huge metal tank of a coffee pot, then refills it with water and ground coffee. While the pot gurgles in delight, she sits down at her desk, shuffling through forms. Her pen always seems to start leaking, but she keeps plowing ahead. By 10:00 when clients start arriving she has blue smudges on her hands and face testifying to her name. She greets each entrant profusely, showering concern and reassurance on them.

Hernando starts a much more solitary day. He slinks into his tiny office setting his computer aglow like an aquarium of secrets. He spends most of the day untangling the mysteries there.

Employees begin filtering in too. Each employee is responsible for five clients; calling them up see to see how they are doing, helping them with little tasks, or some times just walking with them to The Rainbow.

Rita comes in at 11:30, full of ideas.

This Wednesday, as all Wednesdays, is Star Day. Rita has an extensive video library devoted to star related topics. From 11:30 to 1:30 she plays reruns of *Star Trek*. The whole rainbow becomes dark and while the captain of The Star Ship Enterprise confronts dangers from outer space; Rita and Mary pass out popcorn and cool aid while wearing baseball caps with large tin foil covered cardboard stars sticking up from the tops.

At 2 pm Rita and Mary go out for a couple of hours to visit clients, new and old. While the duo are gone, an audio tape called "Starry Night" plays throughout The Rainbow, crickets and owls and strange scratching sounds serenading the clients. Hernando usually steps out of his office on some errand or adventure.

Evening of the Stars begins at 5 p.m. This is the time for movies. Since all movies have stars, the scope of entertainment widens. Ariadne drops over. Not only does she like old movies, but she seems to take a protective interest in the goings on.

7:30, A *Star Is Born* completed, lights flash on, people just wait, hoping that something else will yet happen. Mary begins rinsing out the coffee pot, and clients begin to understand that it is time for them to return to the isolation of their own apartments.

Ariadne watches the last client depart as Mary tips the big metal coffee maker upside down on a towel to dry. Now that everyone has gone except those two, quietness settles into The Rainbow.

Mary looks up from her completed task with a sense of satisfaction. "Um, Ariadne, I'm glad you let us use this building. Did you and Roy always live in that big house?"

Ariadne stands still for a few moments. "Well, to tell the truth, once I had a very different life."

She sits down and Mary follows suite. Time has a way of pausing around Ariadne.

"I was married to another man. Not a bad man, although you couldn't have convinced me of that back then; he was just very limited." She rests both of her hands on her lap and looks out into the distance. The whole room opens to listen.

"Somewhere after the first several years of marriage he started looking at me in some new way that I didn't understand. He looked let down, down right disappointed. I'm not sure up to that point in my life if I had ever really disappointed anyone before. I was pretty and smart and popular, seems like the apple of everyone's eye. Maybe there were people who had more complicated feelings about me, but they just didn't count, so I thought.

Looking back, I can see that I was pretty limited too. When that man who had been my husband took away his admiration from me I spun off balance like a rug was pulled out from underneath me. I tried all sorts of desperate maneuvers to win his attention back: dressing sexier, cooking better, talking more cleverly, but still that same sad sometimes mean face greeted me after his day of work; granted that there wasn't a whole lot going on inside of me at that time. Finally I landed smack dab on my ass as he walked out of the door for good. Although at that time it sure didn't feel like it was for my good.

He didn't even take his clothes; I think he thought they were contaminated by disappointment. The next few months are pretty blurry for me. I know my son Tommy kept going to school; I must have done all right there. I vaguely remember making baloney sandwiches for his lunch and heating up cans of Spaghetti O's for supper, but that's all I really remember. I was watching television, seems watching television was all I really wanted to do. Well, I was watching this program called Queen for a Day. These sad tired women would all compete with each other to see who was the saddest and most tired. The winner of this contest, all droopy and teary would get a bouquet of roses and new kitchen appliances. One Tuesday evening as I was watching this bedraggled woman say that winning this contest was the happiest day of her life, I blew some sort of fuse. That depressed wretch that I was, died, and in its place stood the Divorced Avenger. It felt pretty darn good.

I took all that man's clothes and piled them in

a heap in the back yard, poured charcoal lighter on them, and threw a match. When Tommy came home from school he saw me dancing and screaming around this blaze like tomorrow didn't matter. I probably scared him because he stood there watching for the longest time before running into the house.

As Divorced Avenger I could finally get out of the house and manage a job. Also in no uncertain terms I told Tommy to leave that toilet seat down or I'd fix him so he'd have to sit down when he peed. In my spare time I had a bag of tricks that made me feel better. My favorite was to sneak into Men's Rooms, peek under the stall doors to make sure there was at least one pair of shoes with pants around it. Then I'd spring the fire alarm. I could just picture those men hobbling out of their stalls scared shitless. Serves them right, or at least so I thought.

One day I found a real ripe bathroom at the Greyhound Bus station. There must have been six pairs of shoes in those stalls so I didn't examine them too carefully. I was too excited. I sprung the alarm. I saw a boy run out of the bathroom with a frantic look on his face. He looked at me and just stared, like those deer that guys go hunting for at night. They shine their car lights into the woods; a deer stands frozen staring into the radiance as its chest gets blown out. That's how Tommy looked as I blew out his heart.

I took his cold hand and we walked out of there. It's funny how he didn't talk about it. I slipped into numbness, not ready for a change of heart, but no longer the Divorced Avenger. I didn't complain about the toilet seat anymore because Tommy was peeing on it anyway. In fact he was peeing almost everywhere--in bed and in his pants sometimes. I got that ex-husband of mine to cough up enough money so I could bring Tommy to a therapist regularly. It wasn't just the peeing, but Tommy seemed so far way all the time.

Things weren't right yet for him or me. I wasn't any man's wife, I wasn't the divorced avenger, and I was just this ex beauty queen who was doing a terrible job of raising a son. It seemed like whatever I did, things got worse.

One afternoon I was cleaning out the basement, it seemed like the one thing I could do that made sense. Hanging up next to the work bench was this beat up but still really warm parka. I remembered it was Ben's; that's my ex-husband's name. Somehow seeing that old jacket that Ben wore a million times, reminded me of everything I had lost. The next day, driving to work, I glanced at myself in the rear view mirror. It was like I was looking at someone else's face. I can't exactly explain it, but I saw myself as if from a distance. It wasn't a bad face, or a bad life behind the face, but that story wasn't me. It wasn't important, but I was…am, not in the way I used to think. I wasn't special that way, but I was here, here and that is important. The dread that had probably been following me around for a long time, didn't matter anymore. It wasn't important.

I had been afraid to be sucked down into dread

and just disappear. I'm smarter now, not because I'm so clever, but because I know that life happens to everybody, not just me. We do our best to stop it, but finally life happens to us all. Now when I see people kicking or hollering or crying or bragging or just plain blank I know that life's happening to them. I can hear it like a grinding sound.

As Mary locked up The Rainbow that night, she thought she faintly heard a kind of grinding sound from somewhere close.

Chapter 26

One morning, Mary has an idea. With the determination of an arctic explorer, she calls Hernando and says that she is going to walk to work. The Blu residence is stuck like an afterthought at a right angle to railroad tracks to the west side of the city on the poorer side of Fernwood.

She steps out of her home on this fateful early morning, heading east, past street corners where children are waiting for school buses, past convenience stores that are just opening, and eventually to a scruffy passage of land along the railroad, not exactly a park, that leads to the general direction of The Rainbow.

This vacant corridor has served as a perfect place for dumping rubbish. At night people back their sneaky cars into the passage way and push trash into this waste land. This is a kind of place that most people would rather not notice unless they are trying to get rid of something. Even after several signs are posted saying "NO DUMPING," occasional plastic garbage bags still erupt along the way.

Wild plants, though, as if passing on the word to each other, have begun depositing hardy seeds here, perhaps at night also. Crab grass and dandelions led the migration. Then purple vetch began popping up between rusty cans. The flood gates then opened to white achillea and purple loose strife. Dainty yellow flowered potentillas crawled over the garbage. White, wild morning glory with hints of pink on hot days covered the gravel along the tracks. Mullein with its pale hairy leaves set up four foot tall yellow flowered sentinels. Stray violets and day lilies, purple and orange in season marked the tracks. As a poignant touch, a few patches of five foot tall Great Blue Stemmed Grass reawakened the memory of the long gone prairies. Above this all an old wizard of a cotton wood tree stretched its furrowed arms beckoning the seasons. Mary can feel the plants stirring under her feet.

On this journey her destination is not a sure thing, but rather a direction, something that can be modified as if the locus of movement is indeed inside herself. Thirty minutes into her trip, she notices a street skirting this wild passage. She veers towards it stepping through a patch of scraggily wild asters. There up ahead is Fernwood Ave. She pauses for a moment before she steps out into civilization taking a moment to wonder about things.

This very evening, the fall night darkening the

windows of The Rainbow, Hernando glances up from his computer. "I'm divorcing Mona."

Mary stops what she is doing attempting to fan the coals of his expressiveness by her attention, to no avail--click, click, and click.

For a moment Rita looks like a virgin on her first longed for wedding night. "Hernando, I know it's hard, but it's for the best. A man like you needs a woman with spark and vision." She waits demurely for his response.

While keys still click, Hernando looks up. "Two women, there's two women I'm seeing. One's a veterinarian and the other is a cute beautician."

Rita recoils; the soft blue berries of her eyes freeze into cold pebbles. That little crevice between her eye brows sends out a code of threat.

Mary picks up the disappearing loose end. "Wow, Hernando, is it hard to figure out which one you like best?"

Hernando winks his eye. "They don't know about each other. I see them on alternating nights."

This marks the beginning of Hernando's silk shirt phase. Every Tuesday night girl friend number one, Gail, meets her Hernando at the office. Every Wednesday evening girl friend number two, Jane, also calls on her Hernando. Both take every opportunity to corral sympathetic Mary. Each express concern about the long hours Hernando has to work and say that he is the best thing that ever happened to them. Like some courting tropical bird, Hernando arrays himself in silken shirts of rainbow hues. To further heighten his romantic impact he begins dying his hair a lovely golden color.

Hernando also joins The Fern Club, languidly inhabiting the exercise room attired in sporty outfits, escorting Gail or Jane to the elegant, expensive soirees meant to entice glamorous, affluent professionals. Except for the slight hunch of his shoulders and an inability to look people in the eye, he is the perfect image of a middle age man trying to look like he is thirty; a man who has finally made it.

Mary watches this metamorphosis wistfully. In budding moments of insight she begins wondering about her life, actually noticing how she seems to be afraid so much of the time. Why can't she spread her wings and fly too? For a moment she feels something very close to excitement, almost like wind in her face. Then some inner sense of flaw creeps in and once again she tracks a weary path of making everything all right for everyone else.

Even the stars sentence her to confinement. Under Belinda's influence Mary has now started reading astrological predictions. The daily newspaper is a new addition to the Blu household; Belinda feels impelled to check out the employment ads again. On December 1, 1992, Mary checks her prediction for the new month. "As a Libra, you can cash in on your empathy. Of all the signs, you are most likely to do what's best for everybody, and get paid for it. Your special talent is to figure out an angle that allows you to get your way while helping others get their ways too. These superpowers are now working for you at peek efficiency."

To Mary the miracle of The Rainbow is that somehow even her lumbering form is swept up in the wake of her partners. They are family now. She makes a point of telling both of them, "You guys are really nice; I don't know what I would do without you." When she walks home that night she hears the high honking sound of geese fleeing the Northern Hemisphere.

Chapter 27

At 2:00 AM Rita picks up the notebook by her bed. Rita's diary: December 5, 1995. Hernando, Hernando, how can you do this to me. I've waited so long for you to be free. Why can't you see me? All I can do is fucking eat brown rice. No matter how pure my blood gets, no one ever loves me, me!

Those two don't appreciate how much I work at night. Somebody's got to figure things out. Hernando has shown his true colors, and Mary is up to something. I feel it. I think she has designs on Hernando, Miss Goody Two Shoes--kiss my ass. I can tell by that silly smile on her face that she thinks those messages I leave her on the answering machine during the night are ridiculous. "My Rita, what a lovely shade of red you have on today." I leave important information and she gives me a fashion commentary. And then damn Mimi won't leave me alone.

I was talking with that guy from the shadow

group--what's his name? I am forgetting so much lately. He said that I'm working real hard and that I'm valiant. For some crazy reason, I started to cry. When someone actually appreciates me, all I can do is cry. I asked him to hold me, but he said that might get things mixed up. If only Mary and Hernando would appreciate me. Nobody ever wants to play with me.

He even says that I'm working with all my not inconsiderable intelligence to find a way to reach people. He doesn't make sense sometimes though. First he says that it's wonderful that I'm expressing my anger and then he says I should look for doors instead of blasting through places. How dare he accuse me of that! I never get angry; it's just people don't listen to me, like that idiot, Mary. My God, my God, nobody will ever care about me; they'll just say, my, my Rita, what a lovely dress you have on. Mary's taking over my company, I know it. My partners are fucking me. They pretend like their taking care of me, but I know it, I know it, they're fucking me!

Chapter 28

"Hello."

"Hello."

"Is this Belinda?"

"Yes, who are you?"

"I'm Mimi, you know, don't you, Rita's girl."

"Oh yes, Mimi, Mary's talked about you. She says that she hopes she can meet you some day."

"That Mary says a lot of things."

"It's so nice of you to call, do you want to talk with Mary?"

"No, I don't want to talk with Mary, I want to talk with you. My mommy says that you're the really smart one over there, and Mary just hogs up all the attention."

"In school I was the smart one. Even though I am a year younger, I used to help Mary with her algebra, but she's a really good sister. We take care of each other."

"Can I be your friend, Belinda? I'd like to play with you. Mary doesn't even have to know about it. We can be secret friends, just you and me--not Mary."

"I suppose Mary wouldn't mind. Do you like book clubs Mimi?"

Mary comes home that evening more uneasy than usual; the more she tries to be nice to Rita the more Rita gets upset. Mary tries not to think about it all on the way home; even in winter that wild passage draws her attention. The clump of tall blue-stem rises like a great fan over the mounting snow. When she does arrive at at that dead end house, she notices that a section of the eaves along the right side of the house has been ripped down by a huge icicle that had been lengthening for days. She wonders if she should tell Belinda about it. After all, it is her house, too.

Mary enters the door to find her sister very busy. She has just painted a purple stripe on the living room door, tied a feather to a dining room chair, and placed a hand written poem in the broken blender.

Hi Belinda, "I was going to talk with you about something."

A look of panic shatters Belinda's face.

Mary stops in her tracks, smiles reassuringly at her sister and decides that Belinda probably wouldn't notice the eaves until spring. Mary quickly tries to think of something less dangerous to talk about, and chances upon that very topic she has been carefully avoiding. "Belinda, I feel sort of funny about Rita sometimes. She hasn't gotten real mad at me for a while, and I know she really does like me, but sometimes I feel real tense about work. I know everything is going to be all right, but still..."

"You didn't make another medication mistake did you Mary? What'll happen to us if you do that again? You're so lucky Rita got you into that business. I think you should stay for a while."

Mary notices how Belinda is tightening her fists up in balls. She'll have to try to reassure her sister more. "Ya, you're right Belinda I suppose I am really lucky. You're a really good sister to remind me. What did you do today?"

"Do you think I'm really smart Mary?"

"Sure, you were really smart in class, and all those books you read...you didn't join anymore book clubs did you Belinda?"

"You're always telling me what to do Mary!" Belinda spins around in her night gown and flies upstairs, leaving her bewildered sister behind.

Perhaps it is the ebbing light of winter, but Rita's visits to the office become increasingly rare. When she does come in she bristles. "Do I have to do every god damn thing around here? I shouldn't even have come in today; I feel so shitty. Those adzuki beans did me in last night." Like a whirlwind she spins around the office, papers scattering. Hernando continues blankly punching keys; Mary is on a reassurance priority alert. "It's so good to see you Rita. That is such a pretty black dress you have on."

Rita suddenly looks vague, as if caught in the eddy of her own whirlwind.

Mary knows that this is a crucial moment. Rita might begin confiding in her, accelerating hostilities, or resuming her work day--for Mary the last option is the happiest outcome.

Rita surfaces. "Do we see new clients today?"

Mary heaves sigh of relief, and so starts one of those afternoons of ragtime grace between the partners. Somehow in spite of themselves they find a little space to play a game congenial to each and helpful to clients.

Chapter 29

Through the desperate haze of her optimism, Mary begins noticing a problem. Her persistent reassurances begin sounding empty even to her. Even worse, Rita's visits to the office continue to dwindle. Though this cuts down on office stress, Mary is being overwhelmed by work. Mary finds herself juggling tasks frantically: trying to reassure a frightened client by phone, listening to a report from a bewildered employee, and shuffling through a pile of forms that needed to be filled out yesterday. Something uncomfortable is poking at her, not so much from the outside, but from within: some strange stubborn resolution is awakening. She decides to talk with Hernando who she finds sitting by the keys of his computer in a plant like trance. Apologetically she interrupts him. "I'm sorry to distract you Hernando, but I don't know what to do about Rita anymore.

It's not so bad that she misses work a lot, but she's practically not coming in at all now."

"That's Rita."

Uneasy but resigned Mary is preparing to step back into her hamster wheel.

Surprisingly an unsolicited comment issues from her partner of few words. Mary thinks she recognizes just a hint of that soldier who prevented the slaughter of civilians in Vietnam. He looks at Mary with the confidence of valor under fire. "What this company needs is personnel policies. I'll call a meeting."

"Aw Hernando, you'd really do that? You'd bring that up in meeting? It's not that I want to hurt Rita. I really like Rita...but." Mary almost laughs as she basks in the prospect of a happy ending. Rita would understand; she really would.

Hernando commences punching keys after he drops a little note on Rita's desk. "Meet me at The Fern Club this Friday...Hernando."

Rita is thrilled, Hernando must be coming to his senses. She spends several nights trying to think of some brilliant new idea with which she can rekindle Hernando's delicate flame of passion. After two sleepless nights she falls upon an idea so bold and breathtaking that it even crosses frontiers new to her. The Rainbow can start making and selling psychic tee shirts. The idea bristles with opportunities. Why, with some well placed ads in New Age magazines, TR would be flooded with letters from people requesting custom dyed tee shirts. TR's very evolved and accurate psychics, sensing energy waves from the letters would create masterpieces clearly depicting personalized, auric energy. She can imagine Hernando gracefully splashing away at tee shirts, while from a safer vantage point she reads those letters. Hernando will love it! This'll fill his pants!

All swathed in Kelly green she approaches her Friday rendezvous with Hernando. She enters the svelte Fern Club dining room like a siren, but there sitting next to Hernando sits silly eyed Mary.

Rita's little form bristles as she sits down, large hands fisting.

Resolute Hernando takes a large gulp of his margarita and lifts his eyes from the table so high that his gaze completely misses his partners and fastens like a grappling hook to the slowly turning ceiling fan. "We need personnel policies; that's what companies have."

The coil that is Rita begins pulsing with pressure. She sees Hernando following the circular movements of the fan with his head and Mary smiling with a desperately apologetic air. Those two are in on this. "Is this some goddamn accusation?" rings through the dining room.

She realizes that salvaging this situation is up to her now. "Oh Rita, it's nothing about you. It's just that we three are such good friends, but we need to work together too. You do so much Rita, but if we kind of have rules, things would even go better. Both Hernando and I like you so much."

"You assholes are talking about me behind my back! How dare you accuse me of not doing my share! If it weren't for my ideas you two would still be in the fucking holes I found you. You can't get rid of me!" She casts an imperiled but valiant look at the conspirators, and clutches her purse in front of her like a shield. "You worms, I'll get you for this!" She sweeps through the restaurant, a green storm swirling, disappearing through the door.

For a few moments Mary fades in and out of existence. The Hernando now released from the ceiling fan interrupts her panic.

"That went well." He smiles in mysterious satisfaction and then begins once again staring at the slow swirl of the ceiling fan. "I'll pick you up for coffee someday. Be there."

This is all too much for Mary, if she could only pretend that none of this ever happened and that the stubborn resolution inside her had never existed.

The next day Rita, the freedom fighter, begins a two pronged attack. She comes to work early now and watches the clock monitoring if the two traitors arrive at work on time. Resolutely on time Mary is unassailable. Hernando, the rabble rouser, doesn't always make the muster. She lowers the boom. No fickle resolution, this. She reinforces this first strategy by announcing, "You guys aren't working hard enough. We have to hit this fucking thing, even if we have to work nights!" Mary attempts to look calm as she pictures nights crowded in by Rita's free floating demands. Hernando stares into space, that strange smile flickering on his face.

Two days later Rita initiates the second prong of her attack. Hernando has just left to usher Gail or Jane to the Monte Carlo Gala at The Fern Club. Mary is earnestly attempting to make a mental picture of the important forms and messages scattered around her desk before she leaves for the day.

Rita springs from her chair. "Have you noticed that there's something goddamn wrong with Hernando? He sits at his computer fucking spaced out. He's on drugs, I know it. You have to do something about it!"

For Mary this is the end of a hectic day. Not only does her head spin with names and faces of clients calling out in need, but DHS is coming in next week to do a yearly check of TR's records. She feels a kind of stirring from within again, but this time decides to ignore it. She answers timidly, "That sounds pretty hard and all, to wonder if somebody is doing drugs." She complements herself on her sage answer, so neutral.

"You goddamn don't believe me. I can tell. You think you're so smart, you're a fucking ostrich!" Rita explodes in rage.

Chapter 30

Rita's Diary: March 19, 1995...What's this thing I have about passive men? I thought that idiot Hernando had some spark of vision, but now that he's stumbling out of that suburban trap of his, he ignores me for those young little girl friends of his. Mary's a wet blanket hanging on him. Now he's got about as much initiative as a dead fly. Unless he really is taking drugs and sneaking around like some slug in the night. What if he's up to something? And that fucking Mary always trying to make things run smoothly. "Oh Rita, you look so nice today." I know I feel and look like used cat litter. Why in the hell do I get stuck with these worms?

I still go to that Shadow Group, although chicken shit Mary doesn't attend it anymore. The Leader asked me what my father was like. I started thinking about it. My mother was a controlling bitch goody two shoes who always tried to make things look good and who never was good enough for my dad. My daddy said that I was his princess. "My, my, little Rita, aren't you daddy's princess." We went on long car rides and sometimes we stopped at night to look at the stars. Twinkle, twinkle little star, how I wonder what you are. I even got to sleep with him because my mother wanted to sleep alone. That cunt! Daddy told me how sad he was that my mother didn't love him. He said that I was his little jewel box. My daddy loved me, me. Twinkle, twinkle.

I come to work and everything is running too smoothly. I hired Mary to help me, not to fucking smoother me. She's always so careful and acts like she's Hernando's big assed house wife. "Oh Hernando, what a wonderful idea, you know so much about business." I wonder if he's sucking up to her pussy?

Oh my God. They're trying to get me out of the way. That bitch Mary it's all her fault. I can handle Hernando; he needs a strong woman. Mary's playing her own fucking game. Why am I always the one who's left so goddamn alone? Even Mimi would get away if she could. I try so hard, opening up further and further sharing everything I have, then people hurt me real bad and then try to get rid of me. I want to die, but I can't even do that because I have Mimi to look after...the fucking little princess!

Chapter 31

The storm continues to brew. Quick to find a solution to please everybody, Mary starts thinking that maybe one of those lawyers who advertise on television and know how to help people in trouble might be just what the company needs. No reason everybody can't be happy again, even Rita, if she'd just try a little. Mary decides to bring up the idea of a lawyer, but let Rita chose whoever she wants. That would make it better; at least that's what Mary hopes.

Mary brings the idea up to Rita, very carefully.

Rita eyes her suspiciously and then gets carried away by her own good idea. After all this is her idea. "I've spent too much of my goddamn time on this, but a cousin of mine has a friend who knows a lawyer who would be perfect for this company. He's a brilliant man; I know these things. When we talked on the phone I could tell he was very, very impressed by me."

"Oh Rita, how wonderful. I'm so glad you found someone. When can we see him?"

Rita freezes, besieged by a direct question. In a moment of panic she forgets if she actually had made an appointment. "I'll let you know when I'm fucking ready!"

This same day, Ariadne stops by at closing time again. Mary bustles around The Rainbow, cleaning and tidying everything once or twice; Ariadne watches silently. "I appreciate your earnestness, Mary, but do you ever stop for just a moment and wonder about things?"

Instead of pausing Mary's pace accelerates.

Ariadne sits down quietly.

As Mary washes the coffee pot a second time, she looks up, complaining, "Somebody's gotta do this stuff around here."

Ariadne listens, a far off look in her eyes.

Mary accidentally drops the metal coffee pot in the sink; it makes a gonging, tolling sound. She freezes in place and then slumps into a chair hopelessly.

Ariadne continues to sit quietly watching and listening.

Out of sheer determination Mary sits up straight now. "I've got a plan; I know I can fix it."

Ariadne nods slowly. "Sometimes things spin off and become very difficult, even unmanageable."

Mary quickly reassures Ariadne that everything will be all right.

The next day Rita informs her two partners that

the appointment with the lawyer is on the following Monday.

At 12:30 on that heralded day, the three depart from under The Rainbow. Rita and Mary pile into the old Volvo. Hernando, a melody bouncing around in his head, steps into his brand new purple Honda, with all the options. With his golden hair, his blank face tanned to the color of well done bacon, and clad in a lime green silk shirt, he follows close behind. Rita's Volvo with Mary in the passenger seat is in the lead. They enter a downtown parking ramp, winding down and further down, each descending floor packed with cars, finally reaching a depth where walls are moist and cool and the air, dead.

All three step into the gloom. Rita takes the bow position, clearing the path for her uncertain company. As she tastes the ocean spray she knows that this is her moment of glory, a vindication not only for her suspicions, but for a lifetime ruined by men's failures and women's machinations. She sails up the elevator and rams through the final glass door leading to the twentieth floor reception area of Charles D. Mooseberger Esq.

"We've come to see Charles, I'm Rita. He'll know who I am."

The perky receptionist smiles and presses a button. "Mr. Mooseberger, there's a Rita out here to see you."

A deep distinguished voice issues from the mysterious box on the receptionist's desk. "I don't know a Rita."

Rita's confidence shatters in that instant, leaving a very embarrassed little girl in its place.

Mary watches; she guesses that her happy ending is in jeopardy. "Oh Rita, why don't you mention your cousin's name?"

In a timid childish voice Rita says. "Marjorie White is my very bestest cousin."

The receptionist brightly echoes, "Marjorie White is her bestest cousin."

The godlike voice from the mysterious box pauses, "Marjorie White, let me see. I think I remember. Send Rita in."

A slightly deflated Rita creeps into the sanctuary followed by a tentative Mary and oblivious Hernando.

Charles looks bewildered and finally says, "Well, Rita, so good to see you."

All three slip into seats and stare across a huge desk behind which stands a towering man haloed by gray hair. His face shines powerful and protective, a transcendent being, perhaps absent minded, but never the less awesome. Even Hernando's attention is briefly captured.

"Can I help you?"

Rita sits up straight, marshaling her resources. "I want you to check out my company."

Charles looks deep in thought. Then he utters, "Who handles the books?"

Hernando looks up and makes momentary eye contact with the Charles. "We started this company a few months ago."

From behind his desk, he nods absent-mindedly at Hernando.

Rita looks bewildered and then suspicious.

Charles looks at Rita. "Oh yes, Rita. Now I remember. You're a cousin of…what's her name again?"

Rita perks up again. "Marjorie says hello."

Charles nods absentmindedly and restarts the conversation smiling warmly and vaguely at Rita. "How can I help you? I want to do the very best job for you and your company."

Rita basks in his attention. "I have a real mission, for very important reasons I started this company to give support to mentally ill people." Charles starts staring out the window.

Rita begins deflating.

Mary quick to catch Rita and also more accustomed to being overwhelmed, slips into the conversation. "My name is Mary. "It sure has taken off. It's grown so fast, we wonder if maybe there's things we should be doing that we've missed."

The light still radiates through the fuzzy halo of Charles' wise face. He gazes on Mary benignly.

Rita wakes. "I have a real mission, for a whole bunch of very important reasons, I started a company…"

For a moment Mary wonders if this is what they call deja vu, but then realizes that something is wrong, Rita is floundering. She knows she has to act quickly and tries a dangerous, direct question. "Rita, um, it seems to me that maybe you've had some concerns lately. Do you think that this might be a good time to talk about them?"

Frontal attack, man the battle stations. Rita scowls at Mary and then rises to the challenge. "I don't know if Hernando is doing a good job. It's not that I necessarily think he isn't. I goddam hate it when I don't know about things; anything can happen."

Hernando glances over at Charles with honeyed benevolence.

Charles responds to that glance. "Hernando, how is the accounting going?"

"Fine."

"Any problems?"

"No."

"What accounting system are you using?"

"Peach Tree." Hernando looks at Charles like a boy describing something to his father. "I started using it a few months ago. I plug in the information; out comes what I need. It's real cool."

Charles nods his craggy profile. They are actually making eye contact. Charles glances at Rita with ever so mild censure, "Why Rita, everything seems in order here."

To say the least, this is not turning out as Rita had expected. Not only is Charles not impressed with her valor, but he is actually sympathetic to Hernando. She tries a last ditch tactic. "How do I know that Hernando isn't?..."

Charles interrupts Rita, with a little flick of his hand and then leans back into his deep seat resting in the kind of benevolent wisdom that can laugh good naturedly at any complexity. "What's going on my friends is that you are owners of a company that is fast becoming a big business. Yes, a big business. He stares out the window again saying, "Instead of worrying, you ought to congratulate yourselves and trust each other." Then he stands up and shakes hands with each of the partners.

The three file out. As Mary turns around for one last glimpse of this reassuring vision, she hears that haloed head utter, "Trust each other." Mary feels very safe as she catches up with her partners. Hernando walking with a faint spring in his step, Rita fleeing in confusion; Mary knows just what she needs to do. "Rita that was so brave of you, sharing your concerns like that. I feel proud of you."

"Harrumph!" sputters Rita.

Mary is undeterred. "Do you know maybe what we really need to do, is to spend a weekend with each other. We can just spend the time becoming better friends. Charles seems to think that we have done a pretty darn good job."

"Harrumph!"

Chapter 32

Mary comes home that day, well satisfied. "Belinda, I think I did a good thing today. It'll make everything all right. I just know it." Burgeoning confidence radiates from Mary.

"Mary, Mary quite contrary how does your garden grow? Mimi says that what happened today is stupid."

Mary's head jabs out a little more in something almost like irritation. "How would she know? She's never even been to The Rainbow."

"Mimi knows it's stupid. Mimi knows it's stupid. You don't own me Mary!"

Mary looks confused for a moment. Belinda is the only person in the world with whom she usually doesn't get confused, and now that is changing. Mary decides not to think about it. After all this past winter had been real hard on Belinda. Mary smiles reassuringly. "Did look at your plant catalogs. I know how much you like that."

Belinda glares at Mary. "It's that first shade of green that I can't stand, that horrible lime green color when leaves are just beginning to poke out of the trees. It makes me want to scream." Her arms lock herself tightly within her plaid bathrobe.

Mary shakes her head. "You're going to have so much fun this spring in the garden."

Belinda fastens her eyes on Mary. "I told you I hate green! I hate spring! I hate plants! You never listen to me, you never have. You just think you know me. You don't see anybody but yourself!"

Mary stares at Belinda in complete bewilderment.

Belinda flees up the stairs.

The next day on her walk to work Mary notices that buds are beginning to open on the bushes and trees along her wild way. Angle worms are starting to crawl out of the soft ground to be eaten by robins or squished under shoes. She wonders why things need to eat each other. Funny, how she has never noticed that before.

She tiptoes through that spring and summer. Even when she walks through the changing colored flowers of her abandoned thru way, she feels something looming over her. It doesn't make sense; everything is going so well at the Rainbow. Sometimes she finds her body just stopping as if it were afraid to take another step along that yellow brick road leading to The Rainbow. Even when she sits at her desk, everything seems just slightly out of place.

Unbeknownst to Mary, Rita has started making

frequent nighttime forays into the office to explore the contents of her partners' desks. She knows that Mary and Hernando are up to no good. Mary is such a snake in the grass.

Chapter 33

The fact that the electric fixtures in the upstairs bedrooms of the house on the dead street don't work is less of a concern to Mary than the travail of all those around her. At least that's what she says to herself on that October morning when she finds herself paralyzed in place along her path to work. The falling yellow leaves of the cotton wood tree collect at her feet. With a jerk, her feet again find their momentum and plow ahead.

When she reaches The Rainbow she walks straight to Hernando's desk. His attention is locked to the computer screen as his fingers march over the keys. She watches him for a moment, like a parent gazing at a sleeping child. That's when she notices a drop of red splashed on the keyboard. "Hernando are you all right?"

Hernando looks up, liquid red flowing from his nose onto his golden moustache.

"Hernando you're bleeding!"

"Must be my nose."

"Here, let me get an ice pack and a damp cloth." She bangs around in the kitchen and then comes rushing back, urgency and drama flashing on her face. She ministers to him while offering soothing reassurances. "There, there, Hernando, everything is going to be all right."

Hernando patiently interrupts his work to allow this ministry to take place. Mary wipes the blood off his face gently pressing his head back. As if in reward he starts talking through the wash cloth. "Mary, I've traveled all the spheres of human possibility. I've seen it all and done it all. Sometimes I just wait for the universe to call me to some higher realm."

Not that Mary really understands Hernando, but she is touched by the way he wants to talk with her. She remembers Hernando's blood dream.

Around the corner, Rita silently watches Mary tenderly holding Hernando's head and then flees The Rainbow.

Hours later Rita returns. Though she is smiling warmly, the little crevasse between her eyebrows is flickering. "Mary, you and I haven't gotten together for a long time, and I know that this Friday evening would be perfect. I brought some scotch. Let's you and I stay after work and just chat like old times."

Mary's head nods in acquiescence despite the fact that this is her night to iron her uniforms. She loves to glide the iron over those wrinkly whites transforming them into fresh, smooth promises of a regular, safe future. But this isn't a good enough excuse to frustrate Rita, after all Mary irons just for herself. Yes, Rita needs her.

"Mary dear, we'll spend the whole evening together just getting real close."

Mary's head bobs up and down uneasily. She notices Rita staring in her direction with a particularly tender gaze. Everything will be all right.

5:30 p.m., The Rainbow empties except for Rita and Mary.

Rita jumps up from her desk and scampers over to the kitchen. Mary hears the glugging sound of liquid being poured into two glasses. "Mary, what a wonderful opportunity for us to get really close, really close, no darn men to get in the way."

"What a, what a...good idea, Rita. Just a teeny bit of scotch for me."

"You're so careful, aren't you Mary, virgin Mary?" Rita picks up two glasses each with scotch four inches deep. "It'll make you feel good Mary, you just wait and see." Rita walks over to Mary's desk and places the two glasses on a pile of papers. With a little skipping motion Rita jumps up and perches on the corner of Mary's desk. Those little eyes shinning from under the black bangs, hang above Mary like stars.

"Oh thanks, Rita."

"So nice to see you finally relax Mary, and let your hair down." Rita watches closely as Mary.

With a conciliatory smile on her face; Mary picks

up the drink and takes a large swallow. Her eyes open wide in surprise and then squint in discomfort as she violent coughs, splattering scotch over her piles of paper.

"Oh Mary, you need to be more careful, you'll ruin those papers, and then where would we be?"

Mary sits there. a limp ball of embarrassment.

Rita places a hand on Mary's head. "I'll show you how to do it. What are friends for anyway? Now, first take a deep breath. Then chug the drink down. It'll burn but don't take another breath until you feel the warmth in your stomach."

Mary follows orders. This time, though her eyes are squinting in discomfort, she follows the procedure.

"Now that wasn't so bad, was it?"

Mary nods reluctantly.

"Let's try it again. You have so many hidden talents Mary, don't you? You're quite the operator, aren't you?"

Mary's eyes dart from corner to corner of the room as if looking for an exit. She takes the drink in her hand, breathes deeply then swallows the whole drink.

Rita's face now hangs above Mary like a whole spinning night sky.

"Mary, how are you and Hernando getting along? I'm sure you two have all sorts of lovely little conversations."

"Ahmmmm...Hernando...Ahmmmm.

"You can tell your old friend Rita, and get things off your chest. You'd like that wouldn't you?"

"Ahmmmm...chest...."

"Mary, goddamn say something!"

"Gotta go home...feel funny." And with single minded determination Mary lifts her tall swaying form out of the chair stumbling to the exit. "Sorry, Rita...sorry...tomorrow."

A cold October wind has frozen puddles along her way. Unsteadily she almost slips once, twice and then finally realizes that she needs to take small baby steps. The stiff brown grass chatters as the cold gusts of wind brush through it. A still voice within keeps whispering with the grass, "What is happening? What is happening? What is happening?" By the time she reaches her home, she is too distracted by her concern for Belinda to listen to that voice any more.

Her sister is putting finishing dabs of color on a large tree branch lying in the living room.

"Mary, wouldn't this look good hanging from the ceiling? It'll even camouflage the hole."

"Ya sure, Belinda...the hole in the ceiling?"

"The toilet upstairs is leaking. The ceiling got wet, and there it is." She points nonchalantly at the pile of wet plaster on the living room floor.

Mary numbly stares at the damp pile and then at the hole in the ceiling.

"People put such boring things in their homes. I saw this lying in the back yard and knew it would be perfect for the ceiling. I've been reading this new book on house decorating."

"New book?" Even through the blur of alcohol, Mary's face tightens.

Belinda makes a pre-emptive attack. I wouldn't complain if I were you after what you did."

The phone rings on cue. With blurry frustration Mary picks it up. "Hello."

"Hello."

"Hello."

"Hello."

"Stop it. Who is this?"

It's Mimi. I'm so worried about what you did to my mommy. She said you left her all alone when she was so sad and lonely. She needed somebody to talk to and you just left her there. I'm afraid mommy will hurt herself, and it'll be all your fault."

Mary shakes her head numbly, "I like your mommy so much and would never want to hurt her."

"If I were you Mary, I'd keep trying to call her tonight and make sure she's all right. You were a stinker tonight Mary, a real stinker"...click.

Face flushed, too embarrassed even to look at Belinda, Mary calls at 8PM, 8:30, 9:00, 9:30, and every half hour until midnight. Finally Rita picks up the phone.

"Hello."

"Oh Rita it's you, I'm so glad."

"Who in the hell else would it be?"

"Are you all right? I was so worried about you."

"I was out...with Mimi."

"I'm so sorry I didn't spend more time with you tonight. The scotch just really got to me."

"Oh that, I would have had to leave soon anyway."

"I'm so glad you're all right Rita."

"Do you think there's something the fuck wrong with me!"

"Oh no, Rita."

For the rest of the week Mary makes sure that she compliments Rita several times on how well she looks.

Chapter 34

Rita's diary: October 27, 1996...No one ever believes me. I know something is wrong. Mary, sneaky Mary is at the heart of it. Foolish Hernando is licking her cunt and doing whatever she wants him to do. I need to stop them. I can just see Hernando fucking her, sticking that little worm of his in her fat cunt! Is that why she's trying to destroy me? She's finally getting some, and I'm in the way. Oh my God! They're out to fuck me and nobody will believe me. My, my little Rita everything is all right. This won't hurt a bit. You're daddy's little girl. Twinkle, twinkle.

Trick or treat, trick or treat! They're tricking me and Mary gets the treat. That bitch!

Chapter 35

The front door opens and Mary steps into the Rainbow. She places the folder that she had been clutching and lays it on her desk. She opens her treasure with a sense of wonder; it is filled with orange and black Halloween decorations. She picks out a large orange paper jack-o-lantern folded flat. She opens up the accordioned paper and places it on her desk. She then begins to explore her treasure trove picking each decoration out and taping to to the walls of The Rainbow.

Priscilla timidly walks into The Rainbow. She watches Mary taping up decorations then quietly sits down.

Mary doesn't notice her sitting alone but keeps putting up the Halloween decorations.

Hernando slips into the door and silently sits behind his computer. Mary stops what she is doing, looking at Hernando expectantly. She notices Priscilla. "How are you this morning Priscilla?

Priscilla stares ahead, motionless.

Mary busy with her decorations automatically says, "Everything is going to be okay. You'll see," and then rushes into the kitchen door. There are banging sounds from the kitchen as other guests enter The Rainbow. After several minutes the door from the kitchen swings open and Mary rushes out carrying a cake pan. She starts passing out rice crispy bars. Hernando sits entranced by his computer, pecking slowly away.

Two more guests slip in through the door and sit at a card table.

The two men begin playing cards

The first player slaps down his cards,"I won!".

The second player jumps up. "You can't do that!"

Mary looks alarmed by the angry confrontation.

From across the room a woman screams, "You can't do that!"

The phone begins ringing.

A person watching television starts screaming, You can't do that!"

Mary stands motionless, frozen in place. She jolts and runs toward the phone caught in a whirlwind of panic.

From the distance Priscilla watches. In a shear act of will, Mary calms her face. "This is Mary Blu at The Rainbow Mimi's voice answers, "Mommy says that you hog all the attention."

Mary's face flashes in anger. "Why isn't your mommy here?!"

The sound of Mimi hanging up echoes in the receiver. Mary suddenly looks ashamed and confused. Angry voices fill the room.

Hernando looks up from his computer calmly. "I want more coffee."

Rita rushes through the door into The Rainbow, a cell phone in her hand. "Do I have to do every goddam thing around here! I shouldn't even be here today, the way I feel.

Mary and the pan tumble to the floor. The pan hits the ground gonging and gonging like an alarm.

Rita looks down at Mary contemptuously. "Blu, if you had half a brain, you'd be a halfwit."

Mary crawls across the floor picking up rice crispy bars muttering under breath, "I'm sorry, I'm sorry, I'm sorry."

Hernando obliviously says, "More coffee."

Rita sees him and sidles over to his desk and in a childish voice says, "Are you a bad daddy?"

Hernando smiles at her and says, "Daddy loves only you."

Rita stares at Hernando and in a adult voice says, "You better keep it that way!"

Priscilla watches in a kind of paralyzed trance, and stands up, walks to the door, quietly opening it and steps out of The Rainbow.

Chapter 36

A witch and a goblin and a skeleton are walking back to Thorndike Towers late that night, each grasping a crackling brown paper bag half filled with Halloween candy. A hard, smacking wind threatens to flap away their gruesome clothes leaving three small children desperate to hold on to their meager treasures. As they face the wind and turn off the street towards the shadowy mounting towers of their home, a single ghostly figure is slipping out of those dirty glass doors.

The three children grasp their bags more tightly as the apparition flees by them. The skeleton rattling with cold or fear whispers to the witch, "Did you see her spooky face?"

The wind pushes that ghostly figure onward, her eyes exploding in terror. Each gust swirls her streaming hair forward until it forms a brown tendrilled cave out of which the phosphorescent pallor of her face gleams.

Pushed along that other end of Fern Avenue like litter, impelled by the tumult of that night, she is finally forced up against the railing of the Fern Avenue Bridge. A dark river mumbles secrets underneath. She stands against the railing mesmerized by the flowing water beneath her. She lifts one leg and then the other over the railing. She stands now on the ledge, her back to the railing, and the wind streaks through the tresses of her hair. Those exploding wild eyes of hers close. After a moment so still that the entire city pauses, her form leaps into the sky, sailing downward without a sound.

Chapter 37

The energetic growth of The Rainbow is tapering off. No matter how many new clients enjoy the temporary safety of that shelter, no matter how many cups of coffee and rice crispy bars Mary serves, payroll keeps becoming more difficult to make. Even Hernando says he doesn't understand it, but he has a lot on his mind. Last evening at the Halloween Extravaganza at The Fern Club, while Hernando dressed in a pale suit danced with a pert partner to the sophisticated strains of Ron Borcowitz's Band Divine under the twinkling ballroom lights, someone noticed and then ignored what looked like drops of blood scattered across the floor. When The Band Divine finished and Hernando turned to go back to the table, his partner screamed. Indeed the rear of those pale trousers was stained crimson, like some dramatic poinsettia centered on his rectum. With a blank face he follows the lead of his new girl friend across the dance floor and out of the reach of the stunned whispers of the beautiful club members.

The day after this event, while Mary is walking around The Rainbow telling clients and employees that this really won't be such a bad winter, she hears the phone ring and frantically rushes to her desk to answer what might be someone's call of need.

"The Rainbow, this is Mary Blu, can I help you?"

"Mary this is Jean Harte, I'm Priscilla Emerson's social worker. She had told me many times how much she loved to go to The Rainbow. She said that she always felt as if she really wasn't strange there. I wanted to let you know that there will be a memorial service for her tomorrow at Mercy Hospital Chapel. She jumped off the Fern Avenue Bridge last night."

There was silence on Mary's end of the phone except for a kind of muffled swallowing sound. Each time Mary opened her mouth nothing came out.

After listening to several gulps Jean quietly said, "I'm sorry, Mary."

That day while passing rice crispy bars, the picture of Priscilla plunging in to the dark river tears reassurances out of Mary's mouth leaving her standing silently, swallowing.

Fortunately Hernando's pressing needs are thrust again into the forefront of her attention. That afternoon she notices that Hernando is making very frequent trips to the bathroom. The bathroom and Mary's desk share a common wall. She begins listening for the flushes. Often on his return trip to

his desk he pauses a few seconds in front of Mary
and then marches on. By the fifth pass she realizes
that he either has a urinary tract infection or wants
to speak with her.

Mary finally attempts to solve the riddle during
his last pass at her desk. "How's your week going
Hernando?"

"Okay." Stopped in some kind of neutral he now
stations himself motionless in front of her desk.

His shoulders are giving in to the gravity of his
need. Frantic to prevent his imminent collapse, she tries
a desperate maneuver--she stares into his downcast
face to make eye contact. That face suspended from
his drooping shoulders lifts and turns, not exactly to
Mary, but fairly close.

"I'm having an accident."

"Oh Hernando what happened?"

"Hemorrhoids."

"Hemorrhoids?" She recalls that ominous blood
dream and shivered.

He nods.

"Can I do anything for you Hernando, really can
I? Oh Hernando, hemorrhoids!"

"I'm all right now."

Just when she is about to reassure him, she finds
herself gulping again as if somehow she is trying to
keep something down.

"I don't have a girl friend anymore. Next week
I'm going to fire walk."

For once, Mary is at a loss for words

Faint animation flickers on his face. "Fire walking is when you take off your shoes with a whole bunch of people, and then everybody sings and dances around and you walk over glowing hot coals barefoot. It's very spiritual."

Mary is alarmed. "But Hernando, you might hurt yourself!"

"It'll be okay. I learned this trick a long time ago. I don't feel anything. I just tell myself nothing's real so I can do whatever I want. Nothing hurts me." Hernando returns to the web of his computer.

There are other signs of trouble at The Rainbow; perhaps even luck is running out. If you stop very quietly for a moment you can almost hear the whirring sound of dread. When Ariadne steps in the door that afternoon she stills her gray head for a moment and just listens, as if to some familiar melody.

Charlie, one of The Rainbow's first clients, has started barricading his apartment door again, screaming warnings out of his opened windows. After a stable respite of a year, he is being committed again to the state treatment center. And then there is Priscilla...

Ominous sounds are also rumbling from the state legislature and from Congress. Funding cuts are in the air. Politicians with earnest faces, innocent of awareness, smile as they create new plans for economizing. Dread peeks out of their confident faces as they scramble to catch the latest wave of hysteria that ripples through their electorate.

Mentally ill clients find themselves are running for cover. Rita, no longer satisfied looking through Mary and Hernando's desks at night, discovers waste paper baskets and begins mining that rich vein. Hernando begins coming in at the break of dawn exploring the racy frontiers of the Internet. At times Rita and Hernando only miss each other by minutes. Mary accelerates at a frantic pace; scrambling through mountains of paperwork and washing dishes. She is strangely silent, though. A vague restlessness filters through their employees. Many of them begin considering new occupations or even going back to school. Clients...clients begin to wait for something more to be taken away.

Chapter 38

One Saturday morning that November, well before Belinda wakes up, the phone rings at the Blu household.

"Hello?"

"It's Hernando."

"Hi, Hernando."

"I'll be by in twenty minutes." Click.

"Okay." Quietly Mary prepares herself and then edges down the complaining stairs. At exactly 9:30 on a listless November morning, Hernando's very quiet car stops in front of the decaying Blu home.

Mary slips out the door and into the car with a vague sense that something is different. "Hi Hernando."

"See my new car?"

Sure enough, when Mary looks around she notices that the car is a different color, a crimson red. In spite of the pounding punk rock some little part of her can't just ride along in the mystery. "But Hernando, what happened to your other new car?"

"This one's crimson!" And he begins demonstrating all the accessories: sun roof, leather seats, air conditioning, and most important, a top of the line sound system. He smiles vaguely but blissfully. "Great isn't it?"

Mary stares at something indistinct but frightening in the distance.

As Hernando's flaccid features nod back and forth with the beat, he spins his car around on that dead end street and screeches off.

Mary keeps swallowing over and over again as if something inside can no longer stay down--Hernando is spending a lot of money. Even if he were a whiz with credit cards, buying a new car because it was crimson seems, well, extravagant. She finally stops swallowing; she has an idea. Maybe that bleeding dream of Hernando's isn't just about himself but the company. Hernando is bleeding the company. For a moment she shudders and then resolutely decides that perhaps he is reaching out to her for help. Why else would he show her his crimson car?

She begins picturing a happy ending. Hernando has a problem and she and Rita will see to it that he gets help. He can grow through this difficulty; all three partners can, and they can still live happily under the rainbow. Mary is tentatively smiling by the time Hernando deposits her back at her own home.

With the determination of Dorothy, she calls Rita's home.

"Hi Rita."

"What do you want?" Rita has just come home from a late night at the office exploring desks and waste baskets.

"We might have a little problem."

"You're telling me?"

"Hernando stopped by earlier this morning. He has a new car; ah, I mean a newer car. He got this one because it was red. I think he's got some kind of problem."

"You goddamn think he has a problem. It's about time you got your head out of your asshole!"

Mary is beginning to wonder whether talking to Rita is really such a good idea, but if this is going to be a happy ending she needs to push on. "You were so smart Rita to wonder about this stuff before. It might be a really good idea to have an accountant come in and check things. If Hernando has a problem I guess I want to know about it."

"If Hernando's got a problem, you've got a problem."

"I know I should have listened to you more, but maybe things can still work out for us. I'll ask that we hire one of those, um…accountants to maybe check things out. I'll figure out a way to bring it up at our next meeting." The image of Hernando's soft mouth opening and closing stokes the fire of her determination. It was only after she hangs up that she starts to wonder if she might have betrayed that wounded man. What if he really is honest and she is increasing the burden of suspicion on those sagging shoulders. She would have to think of some way to propose getting an accountant that wouldn't hurt Hernando.

Each day her will to action is further eroded by doubt. And Friday comes, drinks and hostile silence at the Fern Club dining room with her partners. Mary reluctantly takes charge. "You know, I was talking to a friend of mine who knows a lot about business things. This person thinks that The Rainbow is growing be leaps and bounds. He really thinks that such a fast growing company should have an accountant come in and maybe see that everything is running smoothly. I know you put so much work in, Hernando, and you do such a good job, a real good job, but I wonder if maybe it might make sense to have someone, well you know what I mean."

Rita smiles coldly.

Hernando stirs slightly, his voice tinged with disappointment, "If that's what you want, I'll look for an accountant."

Mary doesn't know which of her partners is more deserving of her apology. She walks home that evening under the weight of remorse, finally reaching her dead end home.

As she enters, Belinda plunges down the stairs in her swirling bathrobe. "Mary I have...I have wonderful news. Mimi called me last week and told me about this job I can do at home. I don't have to leave the house! I'm now a proud employee of Metro Market Information. I'm doing telephone soliciting. They sent me an application last week. They let me know today I can start working. It's wonderful Mary, wonderful! I HAVE A JOB!" I just need to pay them $50 to cover the expense of starting me out. I know it's worth it."

Mary smiles limply. "But where are we going to get the money?"

Belinda stares at Mary defiantly. "It's just like Mimi said, you don't care about anybody but yourself! This is my big chance Mary. Do you hear me?" Her whole body springs up in determination. She races up the stairs slamming the door to her bedroom so hard that the hole in the dining room ceiling belches out more plaster.

Mary watches the new pile of plaster on the floor; first she has betrayed Rita, then Hernando and now Belinda. She's trying so hard; it just isn't fair. That night she again makes Belinda's favorite dish, macaroni and cheese from a box. Belinda likes the brilliant yellow colored powder that turns into an even more brilliant oily sauce when mixed with water. Unfortunately Belinda does not come down that evening.

Chapter 39

In the next weeks Hernando practices an even more stringent economy of movement. Whenever Mary enters his office only slight finger motions and a flashing screen betray animation. Rita seldom enters the office now except for her clandestine visits. Mary increases her pace; her strange swallowing is getting worse.

This day, snow like ashes of flakes fall down from the inert November sky. Mary sees the door from outside opening and she steels herself to smile.

Ariadne walks in; she pauses, listening. "Hello my dear are you all right?"

"I'm okay Ariadne, I really am. It must have a cold or something. It's not important."

After a moment of embarrassed silence Mary looks up.

Ariadne watches her.

Mary stops swallowing. The silence now is very

simple, even a relief. She starts talking now. "Ariadne how come things don't work out sometimes? I mean they just don't sometimes. I thought maybe that when we started The Rainbow that it would be a place where everything would be all right." She starts swallowing again. "I'm okay. Everything is going to be just fine if I keep trying."

Ariadne looks away. "Did you ever think much about rainbows Mary?"

"Do you mean The Rainbow...it's all I think about sometimes."

"No, not exactly, although I can see how much you do here. No, the kind of rainbow that stretches across the sky like a promise, not that kind of making things better promise, but something that calls out to us reminding us about something we have forgotten."

Mary listens, bewildered but patient. After all patience is one of the few things she knows how to do.

"But somehow most people figure that rainbows are some kind of place, some destination that they can reach and plant themselves in the middle of, all happy and safe--some permanent solution, fixed forever. We get so tight and worried about holding on to that kind of rainbow."

Mary nods slowly, just once; she certainly understands mistakes and being tight and worried.

"Rainbows are not places, they are not even up in the sky, Mary, but rainbows are light and water and eyes. When someone thinks they see a rainbow it's really something happening, maybe something happening inside like waking up. You can't hold it or lose it, but just be glad it's there."

Mary listens quietly, not that she exactly understands, but it's a relief to think that things aren't exactly as she has been thinking.

"Sometimes it takes a storm blowing and banging in the dark to wake up whatever it is that comes alive inside."

Mary drops her head like a child caught in an accident. She is only able to tolerate wondering about things so long; once again she starts swallowing. "I'll be all right Ariadne, don't worry. Boy, I have all this paper work I need to do, but thanks Ariadne, really."

One week later at another Friday meeting while non-sectarian holiday tunes reassure happy endings at the Fern Club, Hernando announces that he has identified an accounting agency. "I'm Dreaming of a White Christmas" quiets Mary's apprehension. The holiday season beckons the three partners. The trio come to the last decision that they would ever make together.

The season even seems to have some effect on Rita. "You know how much time Mimi needs during the goddam holidays, let's wait until they're over and then start with the accountant."

Mary is grateful about the postponement. Who knows? Maybe things will be all right.

Hernando smiles. "I'll set it up for January.

Before that variously anticipated event, there is

one last story for the three under The Rainbow, the Christmas Eve party.

While an instrumental version of "Silent Night" plays over the speakers. Rita pounds on the table. "What we fucking need around here is a Christmas party! Not for us of course, but our clients. We have to do it!" She smiles in a swirl of desperate excitement.

Mary timidly nods.

"Hernando, for goddam once you're going to do something; you can arrange it."

"Mary get those invitations out. I want every client to have a goddamn Christmas! I'll make sure things stay on course." Indeed Rita spends the next several nights thinking about the Christmas party. She decides that every client should have one--no two Christmas presents plus a dozen Christmas cookies. That Hernando better make sure it's a full Christmas spread too. No one is going to ruin my Christmas.

When Ariadne hears the plans, she smiles. "That carriage house is perfectly fine, but no place for a party. Why, Fern Hall would be just right. Roy will supply string beans and tomatoes, and I've got an apple pie recipe that is the toast of Tennessee."

Hernando uses the company credit cards to buy all the rest of the supplies. Rita spends the last two weeks in a frenzy to find the perfect wrapping paper. She even momentarily sacrifices her diet to sample pastries at a multitude of bakeries until she finally discovers the perfect cookies. Mary just continues to push ahead to what she hopes will be a happy ending:

each morning welcoming her guests, asking each of them how they are, and then being at a loss for words.

On Christmas Eve there is certainly enough chaos for Rita as she trundles to clients' apartments picking them up in droves, a sense of mission steaming from her urgent little body.

Hernando has rented a van that night. He and his navigator, Ariadne, also set out to bring guests. Hernando and then Ariadne step into the silent van. He turns on the ignition and the interior is filled with a reassuring rumble.

She looks over toward her driver. Her face clouds in bewilderment and then softens as she sees that the steering wheel is smeared with red. "Hernando what happened? Oh my dear man. There's blood on the steering wheel."

In fact the nail of his right index finger is hanging precariously from his hand, painting the wheel red. Only the moment before he had left his finger like an afterthought in the door as he slammed it. Fortunately he was able to tear his finger loose. "The door bit me." He smiles sheepishly.

"Can I help you do something about that? Oh my dear your finger is torn."

"No time. Where's our first stop?"

"You need to go to an emergency room Hernando."

"No!" He guns the motor and sets off into the night.

She watches her driver for a few moments then reaches into her sleeve and pulls out a handkerchief on which is printed a pattern of yellow roses. At the next stop light, silently she picks up his slack hand and gently ties the cloth around his finger.

He hardly notices the handkerchief except when he tries to turn the radio on; the now red stained wad of yellow prevents him from pressing the little button.

Perhaps it is the absence of loud punk rock music, or the presence of a captive audience, but somewhere between picking up the third and fourth guest, blankly he begins addressing the dark windshield. "When I was a kid, I liked to sing, but no one liked music much there. I'd sneak down to the basement with a flashlight and crawl into a big box that the television came in. I'd shine the light on my face and sing my favorite song, 'Hernando's Hideaway.' I kept going down there. Pretty soon I didn't need the flashlight. Then I didn't even need to sing. All I needed was the darkness."

All the occupants of the car listen as his voice disappears into the night.

Chapter 40

A huge, old pine tree sparkling with lights the colors of the rainbow beckon from the spacious lawn of Fern Hall. Car loads of people from the lower end of Fern Avenue pour into Fern Hall. Once inside the hall, a banner with big red and yellow and blue letters spelling "WELCOME" hangs from the ceiling.

At this fete no designer jeans or chic gym clothes are in evidence, only over sized pants safety-pinned closed or shabby dresses. But if you looked closely you could see that everyone has added extra touch of color somewhere to their ensembles, welcoming reds, greens, or even purples. For this one night there is room at the inn.

Roy, dressed in a tuxedo that he exhumed from a third floor closet, meets the guests in the chandeliered hallway. He bows, welcoming them, taking their coats, and telling them to make themselves at home. In the kitchen Mary's frantic body spins from oven, to sink, to refrigerator and back again; bowls, turkeys, pans, potatoes, jello salad, and her own hulking form spins in the cyclone. Soon the guests are seated and served. To Mary's anxious eyes the situation appears dangerously chaotic, but during this evening nothing can go wrong, all is calm, all is bright.

Two guests have panic attacks, another becomes frantically asthmatic and is rushed to the hospital, several of the people begin crying and only copious amounts of food and attention comfort them. They all eat, talk, and get presents.

Then as if a bell has struck, an anxious cloud begins hovering over the conversations and empty plates. It is finished--no longer guests, once again clients, they prepare to return to a world punctuated by psychiatrists' appointments, stark apartments, and form after form to fill out. Mary once again hears the call of dread and begins swallowing. Some vague throbbing from the vicinity of his right hand begins to trouble Hernando. And Rita suddenly sees a pathway of crumbs leading to her hidden, pink box. Mimi who is out of town visiting relatives for the day, is unable to come to the celebration.

Mary sloshes around in the warm dish water as long as she can. Each dish, transformed from dirty too clean, brings the future closer.

When Mary finally wends her solitary way home and steps into her house she is greeted by darkness. In previous years Belinda had decked the halls of that old house with pine branches and tinsel and thousands of little lights. Mary turns on the light, revealing the dilapidated dining room--yes, something hasn't been quite right at home lately. She notices a thin little newspaper called "Meet People" lying on the sofa. She stares for a moment at the smiling young man and woman on the cover so like those beautiful people at The Fern Club. Belinda had carefully circled names and addresses of several men.

Chapter 41

As Hernando promised, the accountant, a Mr. Ronald Grundleboro, steps under The Rainbow at 1p.m., January 15. Mary greets him; the three piece suit and an air of competence are a dead giveaway for someone who surely knows what to do. Perhaps it is the growing sense of something looming, she is beginning to notice things. Mary takes a risk. "Are you Ronald Grundleboro?"

"You can call me Mr. Grundleboro." He stares at her for a moment, just long enough for her to turn away in confusion.

Head bobbing now, she leads him into a side room. She has never actually met an accountant before.

As if some message has passed through secret channels, both Hernando and Rita simultaneously proceed to that little conference room.

Rita, sparkly eyed, looks at him; Mary is looking

down. Neither notice Mr. Grundleboro making momentary eye contact with Hernando.

The four sit down around a table. Muted January light filters through the windows.

Mr. Grundleboro takes charge. "I appreciate Hernando's concerns, and I am here to straighten things out. "He called me several weeks ago to set up this appointment. It's a real privilege to give a hand to such a promising young company." He beams at all three of them in congratulations. Mary blushes, Rita tosses her shiny black hair alluringly, and Hernando stares out the window.

"I'd like each of you to give me your impressions of the company, and then I'll look over the book keeping systems. In three weeks I'll mail you recommendations and a valuation of your company."

Rita jumps in. "I used to know a Randy Grundleboro from high school. Do you have a brother named Randy, you look so much alike."

There is a moment of uncomfortable silence. Ronald Grundleboro and Hernando make fleeting eye contact

Mary fills the gap. "Well Mr. Grundleboro, we don't know very much about accounting."

Rita turns on Mary with outrage. "I know plenty!" Her little eyes narrow and the crevice between them flicker. "I don't trust Hernando. I want someone trustworthy to look at the books and see if we need an audit." She stares stonily at Hernando who now hunches over, a wounded look on his face. Mr.

Grundleboro intervenes. "I'll certainly look into everything very thoroughly." He stares pointedly at Rita for an instant.

Mary looks relieved, "Mostly I just want the company to be okay and people to be happy. I think Hernando has worked very hard, but it might be good if someone checks that everything is all right. Then we can all rest in peace."

After a few moments of silence everyone in the room turns to Hernando.

He smiles innocently. "I think things are running smoothly, but if people want to check that, it's all right by me."

Mr. Grundleboro smiles at all three of his charges. "I appreciate your candor. I'll take all of this in consideration and get that report to you in a few weeks. I'll meet with you again to see if you have questions."

The three weeks grind by; each partner keeps their cards close to their bodies. On Friday February 26th just as the partners returned from their Friday meeting, a messenger delivers three very important looking envelopes to The Rainbow.

Hernando slips into his office with his envelope, Rita ferrets hers away in her purse.

Mary wide-eyed opens hers at her desk. She studies the report carefully. She begins to smile and then looks at the letter more carefully. She looks up, gasping, "This is a big business!" It turns out that Mr. Grundleboro values their business at $300,000.

He writes that rather than audit, the company needs a line of credit.

Never in her wildest dreams did Mary expect to be part owner of such a valuable company. She feels a cool breeze run through her life. She wonders if this is what people call optimism.

For the second time in two years Hernando's role in the company not only survives scrutiny but is praised. A jolt of guilt courses through Mary--what about her suspicions? Perhaps all along she has been subtly fueling the furnace of Rita's anger. Mary's face once again begins pulsing with shame as she wonders how she could have let this happen.

That afternoon she has a visit from each of her partners. At 4 p.m. Hernando limps to Mary's desk. His eyes are red as crushed strawberries. His mouth softly opens and closes.

"I can't stand her suspicions about me any more." Clear liquid begins trickling from those red eyes. "I work hard as I can. I put extra hours in to keep things on track."

The sight of Hernando's face seeping tears, pierces Mary's heart. She sees this valiant Vietnam Vet struggling to maintain his dignity. She knows that she has a part in his pain. "Hernando, it's not right that you have to go through this ordeal any longer. Mr. Grundleboro gave us a clear bill of health. I'm sorry for not stopping this sooner, but IT WILL STOP NOW!" She looks startled by her own fierce determination.

While an expression of tentative gratitude animates Hernando's face, Mary's face begins paling--what is she going to do about this? Fortunately she has piles of paperwork. She stays later than usual that night, after all, when she gets home she can figure this all out.

One hour after closing time, there is a surreptitious click of the door lock; secretive Rita pokes her head in. She and Mary catch each other's startled eyes.

"What in the hell are you doing here?"

"Oh I have all this paperwork to do...I fell a little behind today...ah, I got the accountant's recommendation. Looks like everything checked out."

"Goddamn accountant! This time I have proof that Hernando blew it, and blew it bad." She looks to Mary for reinforcement.

With new found determination, Mary looks at her blankly, no reassurance here.

Rita smiles with cold contempt. "You're making a big mistake. You'll pay for this, you'll fucking pay for this!"

There is an edge in Mary's voice now. "You know Rita, if there's any problems bring them up at our next meeting. I won't talk behind Hernando's back." Mary turns and leaves the office, a chord of determination vibrating deep inside her.

Chapter 42

Rita's diary: February 7, 1995--I knew I'd find something! I'm not going crazy! I made copies of all the financial records and gave them to Roger Handcock, a very close friend of mine. He's also an accountant. Roger saved my sanity, he found a big mistake. That Hernando's been naughty--I warned that goddamn Mary about it, and she just looked at me like she had a popsicle stick up her ass. She thinks she so smart. I see London, I see France, I see Mary's underpants. And they're fucking dirty. She wants to take over this company. Hernando's incompetent like all men, but Mary the bitch is trying to do me in. If only she'd get out of the way and leave Hernando and the company to me, me. I'd take care of things.

Oh my God, I thought I was slipping down again but this time for good--that goddam bitch!

Chapter 43

No matter how hard Mary thinks on the way home she can't really sink her teeth into an idea for helping Hernando. It is like bobbing for apples. She starts thinking of a big juicy idea, opens her mouth wide and lunges face forward toward her target. Then suddenly she is flooded with apprehension, coughing and sputtering.

She enters her house to find Belinda sitting, reading in the dining room; water drips from the ceiling into a pan making regular pinging sounds. Mary could have avoided noticing this for at least a while, but something too dramatic to be ignored is also occurring--Belinda is dressed up in their mothers green velvet dress, the one she only wore on special occasions. Even more dramatic, Belinda has makeup on.

"Belinda what are you doing?" Mary's mouth hangs open as if waiting to be fed.

For a moment Belinda blushes and then snaps the book on her lap shut. "You just don't want me to look pretty, Mary. You go out and do exciting things and I just stay here getting older. I hate my goddamn poetry. I know somebody who thinks I'm beautiful and someday he says that he'll take me away from here. Besides you better not complain too much Miss Smarty Pants, Mimi said that you made a very big mistake today and that you'll be sorry."

Mary keeps shaking her head and swallowing. "Belinda, you never talk to me anymore, you just get mad at me. Please don't be like this." She pauses and then dangles a memory in front of her angry sister. "Do you remember how we'd sneak into the old coal bin so mom and dad couldn't find us, and we'd pretend that we could fly like birds over the rainbow and go somewhere that was wonderful where nobody is afraid...and that when we'd get there together and we'd take care of each other always no matter what... and everything would be all fine again?"

For a moment Belinda looks like a child longing to go home, but something inside wrestles for the control of her face. Her eyes tighten thin as wires and a voice came out all frantic, clumsy and new born. "Don't you try to stop me Mary, don't you try!" She runs up the stairs, green velvet whispering.

That night Mary eats potato chips and ice cream in the dark kitchen swallowing even when her mouth isn't full. She wakes up the following morning and quietly gets ready for work. After all she doesn't want to wake Belinda; she had a hard night. Mary knows that she must have done something very wrong. Maybe at least today she can help Hernando. After all, he's family too. Maybe even Belinda will forget about the whole thing bothering her...whatever it is. As Mary trudges to work that morning breathlessly waiting for happy endings, she doesn't hear the crows screaming at each other across her snowy path.

That Friday the three partners again meet at The Fern Club Dining room. When Mary arrives she finds Hernando sitting there already, crumpled and like a baby bird, fallen naked from its nest. Rita arrives a few minutes late, glitteringly defiant, bullet earrings banging dangerously.

Mary starts. "Hernando came up to me yesterday; he was crying. He said he couldn't take our suspicions anymore. I feel so sorry for what happened to him and how I had a part. You know we've seen a lawyer and now a real accountant. Everybody says that Hernando is doing fine. I think we have to stop all these suspicions now. Maybe we do have problems, but maybe it's how we treat each other." Mary pauses for a moment, and then smiles as if she has finally bobbed down far enough to sink her teeth into a succulent idea for a happy ending. "I think that we should hire one of those people who help other people learn to talk with each other."

Rita springs out of her chair, one large fist pounding the air, "Fuck it! I know you think I'm crazy. This is just another way to get rid of me. There's a real problem now Miss Smarty Pants. No one is going to send me to a therapist because they think I'm crazy. There's something wrong with the company books. I found it out, I found it out, I found it out!"

The pressure of years of meekness pounds in Mary's ears. She stops swallowing. "We can't hire another accountant; we've just done that! You'll just keep finding things forever to be suspicious about." That pounding now fills her whole head. She looks to Hernando for reassurance.

Avoiding eye contact, he mumbles, "Me, too."

Mary stares at Rita resolutely.

Hernando glances at Mary with damp eyed gratitude.

On Mary's way home, the gray sky breaks open, allowing the stars to shine through. She listens to the crunch, crunch, crunching of her boots as the path leads her home. Her home, her home, Belinda. Whatever is wrong? Mary can surely make it all right for Belinda. Mary will do it better this time and not make any mistakes. She'll take real good care of her sister, real good care, really good care.

Chapter 44

That week Rita remains at home. Hernando disappears into his computer. Mary looks in on him one afternoon. He has the shades down in his office, and he stares at the screen on which "Hernando" is written over and over again filling the whole expanse. He presses the delete button and letter by letter all the "Hernando's" begin vanishing into oblivion.

Friday shortly before the anticipated drama of their weekly meeting, head drooping from his suffering shoulders, Hernando approaches Mary's desk with a registered letter. He looks at his partner, opens and closes his mouth softly, and then passes the letter over to her. Something inside Mary slips and plummets as she read its contents.

"Oh my God, she can't do this Hernando?"

Hernando nods piteously.

"She can't force us to pay for another accountant!"

Hernando nods again.

In all the stress Hernando must have been losing his powers of concentration because he simply begins walking away. As he returns to his computer Mary reassures him. "We'll get through this, everything is going to be all right."

Hernando doesn't reply.

Two days later, six feet of worked out, power dressed, networked thirty five year old male sweeps into The Rainbow like a righteous super hero. Before bothering with introductions he takes over the meeting room as the brain center for his operation. He menacingly spreads the arsenal contained in his briefcase on every available surface. Then he bounds from his operations center on his first mission.

"So you're Mary." He clucks his tongue a few times before smiling maliciously. "I'm Roger Handcock your accountant; you'll be seeing a lot of me."

Mary scrambles behind her desk swallowing rapidly.

He stares at her with righteous indignation as Mary flutters nervously behind her piles of paper. He scans the room as if there were an audience who could appreciate his clever maneuver. After silent applause he heads to Hernando's office.

For the next week Roger makes forays out of his office; drama and chaos following in his footsteps as he prepares for the first starring role in his brawny but lack luster career. His square jawed smiling face with ginger hair cleverly combed forward to disguise a shiny too expansive forehead can be seen popping into all kinds of nooks and crannies with menacing curiosity. When Ariadne drops in he even tries to stare her down; she ignores him.

Chapter 45

Within two days of the invasion, while Rita remains shrouded in mystery, Mary notices that Roger has invited Hernando to assist him. They spend days rummaging through piles of paper. Each day Hernando's shoulders slip closer to the ground. His whole face winks with worry. On the third day while Hernando is out to lunch, Roger invites Mary into that nerve center. He closes the door behind her and smiles familiarly at her. "You've made a very serious mistake here; you have big problem."

Mary's stomach flips over with terror.

Roger pursues his quarry. "Hernando made a very serious mistake, very serious. All of you are going to owe a very large amount in back taxes. His mistake was very, very unnecessary."

As her gulping becomes more frantic, she crumbles into her chair.

He smiles at her viciously, "I know you're such a

busy woman but I want you to sort through some of these papers for me.

Mary doesn't move.

"Now!" Then he smiles at his audience.

Of course Mary doesn't notice the smile; she is preoccupied with a strange whirring sound grinding through her head almost like a melody, a banging melody--a very serious mistake and she is at the center of that dark spiral.

That next day Mary quietly slips out of her home, and after a snowy walk, steps into the office door only to find a very excited Roger waiting for her. His eyes dance. "It's about time you got here Mary--a very interesting situation, very interesting. Your friend Hernando called in with a very sudden case of the flu. Now take this pile of bills and alphabetize by company name."

"Is it very bad Roger?"

"Very, very bad." His eyes dance with pleasure.

"As that grinding sound throbs in her ears again she timidly asked, "Is there anything that maybe shows that Hernando is doing something wrong?"

His smile broadens. "My, you two take such good care of each other, don't you Mary?"

Even though taking care of other people is the thing she does best, that grinding sound gets louder as she nods. "I try my best."

"I'm sure you do Mary. I'm sure you and Hernando take very good care of each other, so to speak."

Mary walks to her desk to drop her coat on her

chair, looks wistfully at the pile of urgent messages on her desk, and returns to Roger's grasp.

Midway through alphabetizing the bills, Roger decides it would be more convenient for him if she would file them by date. Mary barely lifts her head as she complies.

"This certainly is a friendly office Mary. I've never seen such a friendly, friendly office, at least you and your friend Hernando. It's so important to have good friends isn't it Mary--good friends, good friends to do things for each other." He smiles confidentially.

"Ah sure Roger, Hernando's been dependable. I know he made a big mistake; I think he got overwhelmed. I'm friends with both Hernando and Rita."

Roger shakes his head. "Rita is very, very concerned about this company. It's certainly a shame that a smart girl like you didn't listen to Rita. Not that anybody did anything wrong. Did they Mary?" His eyes now fill with dewy innocence. "Mary, Mary, do you always make excuses? Some people make excuses when they have something to hide? Do you have anything to hide, Mary?"

Towards the end of the day, bills almost refiled, Roger lowers his large hand on the fruits of Mary's labor. "Mary there's something in Hernando's desk that I want you to get for me."

It takes a few moments for the muddy stream of bills to cease running through her head. "You know

Roger, I wouldn't feel right going through his desk without asking him first."

"Soooo you wouldn't feel right about going into his desk. How very, very loyal you are Mary."

This time Mary notices the strange smile on his face; she shudders. "I'd like to help you Roger, I really would, but I'd have to call Hernando first."

"You two certainly keep close tabs on each other, don't you Mary?"

"I suppose so."

"I have another little task for you that hopefully won't offend that delicate sensibility of yours."

"Well sure if I can do something..."

"I want you to meet me at Freedom National Bank tomorrow, the bank The Rainbow has its accounts at. You and Hernando must have gone there very, very often."

"Oh sure Roger I know where that is."

"I need bank statements to reconcile some of these figures. After that you WILL get me the information from Hernando's desk!" Without waiting for an answer, Roger snaps his briefcase closed, and charges out of the office grinning.

As the door slams shut Mary's body sags in relief. She lets her eyes stare straight forward out of focus until her life seems like someone else's memory, someone whom she can reassure. Then the pile of urgent messages on her desk beckons her back to her own life. She swallows and realizes that she has things to do and will think about all of this later.

Later that evening as each of her boots scrapes through the snow and the brittle frigid air tears into her nostrils; stars usually unseen except on moonless bitter cold nights wink on and off over her head in startling proximity. For a moment even she notices, but then she has another idea.

Walking into her house; she doesn't notice the desperate straining of the furnace or even the dripping sound from the dining room. She notices something new and subtly different. Looking around with unaccustomed acuteness she sees no signs of branches, feathers, or stray poems; some spirit has withdrawn from that decaying house. "Belinda are you here?"

No answer.

Mary begins exploring, turning on the lights room by room. Funny how now she notices things that she has never seen before: the darkened warping wood of the floors, the walls cracking in the shifting restlessness, the way the single pane windows rattle vulnerably against the cold, the linoleum worn through by her frustrated attempts to make gracious meals. She walks upstairs and hears her steps echo through the empty house.

There is one single yellow light shining, illuminating Belinda's desk in a cone of light. Something is written on the back cover of Meet People Magazine. "Mary, by the time you get this I'll be long gone so don't get frantic about all the things you could have done to stop me. Herman Olson from Juneau Alaska has just parked his van in front of this house.

He's coming to pack me up and take me away. He wants to marry me. That's a funny word, "marry." I feel like I have been "Maryied" all my life. You're my first memory. Even when I was still really tiny I remember this bewildered, tender face looking down on me saying, "Everything is going to be all right my little Belinda, I'll take care of you." And you did. When mom and dad struggled through their life together on this desperate island of a house, you took me on trips to places that were safe...places you made up. But you made up those places Mary, I didn't. Every time I tried to go on my own trip you looked at me with that same bewildered, tender expression, and I just stopped and let you make everything all right. Everything wasn't all right Mary, we were just pretending. Mimi helped me see that. It's not your fault Mary, we did it together. It was me, too.

I'll write you from Juneau when I get settled there.

Your Sister,
Belinda"

Chapter 46

$\mathcal{M}$ary blurs her vision and fades into that empty house. Only the yellow light from what was Belinda's desk keeps nagging her to come back to remember something, something. That's it, that's it--poor Hernando and Rita, someone needs to help them. Hernando made that big embarrassing mistake and Rita, well it must have been so hard for her when she was right and nobody (Mary's face flushed with hot prickles) listened to her.

Mary has another plan of rescue.

With determination she walks to the phone. "Hi Hernando, it's Mary, how are you today?"

"Sick."

Mary senses vulnerability in her partner. This bodes well. "It sounds real hard and I'm sorry you're in the middle of this."

"Never said I was an accountant."

"You must have felt so overwhelmed; did you just panic and not tell anyone how lost you were?"

"Yes."

"I've got an idea. I don't think it's too late for us three to get together. We've all made big mistakes. Maybe we can kind of start all over again, but this time treat each other real nice."

"Maybe."

"So you'll meet with Rita and me? I haven't asked her yet, but if you say yes, I'll call her. I bet she'll do it. She's a good person, but just kind of gets upset sometimes, and she's real smart. Look how she figured out our accounting was wrong. I'll make sure she won't scream at you. No one deserves to be screamed at."

"Ya."

"Oh, one last thing, Roger asked me to give him some of your files tomorrow. If you're still sick, I'll bring those to him."

He makes a kind of humming sound.

"Good talking with you Hernando. Everything is going to be all right. You just wait and see."

Click.

Mary feels warmed by Hernando's vulnerability. The next step will be harder, though; she needs to call Rita. Inspiration burns through her timidity... she wades in the water. "Hi Rita this is Mary, how are you?"

"What do you want?"

"I know I hurt you badly and I'm sorry. You were right about the problem."

"I goddamn was!"

"I feel real sorry for those times I didn't listen to you."

"You goddamn better be!"

"I spent the day with Roger and I know the accounts are a mess."

"Goddamn right."

"I remember how happy we three were to start this company. We called each other family. I still feel that way towards both of you."

There was a pause and a shuffling sound on Rita's end of the phone. A high pitched voice answers. "Oh Mary I'm so hurt. My little heart wants to break. How could you have hurt me like this?"

"It must have been so hard for you. Is this Mimi?"

"My mommy can't talk anymore. You were very bad to her and Belinda. My mommy hurts."

Mary hears the sound of the phone hanging up-- that wasn't so bad. She could make things right again, somehow. Optimism swells in her worried heart. Rita sounds so soft, not the screaming person Mary feared, yes, there is a wounded child underneath just like with Hernando. She, Mary, would protect them both and help them feel safe. She'd help Hernando rise above his embarrassment, and she would listen more carefully to Rita. They are Mary's family now. For a moment she thinks about that yellow light on in Belinda's empty room, and then she focuses on the urgent needs of her partners. Mary crawls into her bed and sinks into sleep.

She wakes early, the winter night still bearing down with cold anguish. The wind bangs at the windows. She softly walks down those creaky stairs, not wanting to disturb...oh ya Belinda's gone. She mustn't think about it. She sits blankly on a dining room chair waiting for events in which now she has a central role. No sun greets her this morning. The dark air is heavy with blowing snow. As the sky turns a chalky, swirling gray she leaves that house on the dead end street to take the bus to Freedom National Bank and her rendezvous with Roger.

Mary leaves the safety of that hot, crowded bus and steps into the blowing snow to meet Roger. Just as she passes through those polished clear glass bank doors, she notices the back of a familiar pony tailed head talking earnestly with a teller. The pink flamingo feather is a dead giveaway. Hernando--but he's sick-- grabs a large pile of what looks like money, something deep inside Mary crashes. Brain in grid lock, her eyes all by themselves fill with liquid as she mechanically walks out of the bank into the swirling morning.

"Pssst...Mary, it's Roger. I tried to stop you before you went in." "Let's hide and watch him. As soon as he leaves the bank we'll explore a very, very serious problem."

Roger's excitement mounts in ecstasy as the two watch Hernando through the bank windows. They watch him rush to his crimson car disappearing inside. He skids out of the parking lot and fades into the snowy blustery day.

The sound of his screeching takeoff jars Mary's numbness for an instant, then she allows the snow to engulf her again.

Roger races toward the bank throwing a gleeful command back over his shoulder. "Come with me, we'll see what your friend is up to."

Mary tries to look like she is capable of agreement and follows.

Eyes glittering he approaches the teller. "This is Mary Blu, an officer of The Rainbow. I'm the accountant, Roger Handcock of Handcock and Company. Did a certain Hernando Mueller withdraw money from the company accounts?" He pierces the teller with his stare.

The cashier winces under his scrutiny, and then musters all the formality of which she is capable. "I need to talk to my supervisor." She retreats for reinforcements.

One minute later a composed and very official older woman speaks with our duo. "I need to see identification."

Roger glances at Mary. "Show your identification!"

Mary does and then backs away.

The older woman cautiously examines Mary's identification and then reluctantly takes on her role in this drama. "I'll check in back. She disappears for several minutes and then abruptly returns. "Mary Blu, since your name is also on the account, I can share this information. Hernando Mueller has cashed a check for ten thousand dollars. This check was co-signed by you, Mary Blu."

Mary looks on blankly. She vaguely understands that there is some sort of problem and that the problem involves her signature.

Roger scrambles forward. "Let me see that check! I'm the accountant."

The bank officer looks at Mary standing in the distance.

Mary numbly nods.

The officer waves it in front of Roger's face.

He focuses on the moving target, eyes in a climax of excitement. "Is this or is this not your signature Ms. Blu?"

She gazes at the waving paper from a swirling distance until she realizes that an answer is demanded. "Um, I don't think so."

"What do you mean you don't think so, look again?"

"Um I don't think so, I don't make my `B' like that." And then she begins wondering if maybe she is in on whatever Hernando has done. The snowstorm in her mind howls.

Roger's indignation mounts. "Give me a copy of that check now!"

The bank officer disappears behind a partition and after a few minutes of conversation with her superior, she returns and coolly hands a copy to Roger.

He heads toward the door. "Come with me!"

Mary does.

They speed to The Rainbow. Rushing into the door, Mary in tow, Roger smacks his lips as he picks up the phone. "Rita we've got them. Come to the office." He turns his sharp gaze on Mary. "We have a very serious problem here, very serious. Let's see what else we can find in this cozy office. So you're not sure if that is your signature…" He narrows his eyes at Mary and races towards Hernando's files.

Automatically Mary begins fixing the coffee pot.

"Mary, get in here!"

She follows the distant command of his voice.

Hernando's computer screen shows his name printed over and over again.

Roger glances at the screen then focuses on a sheet of paper on the desk.

"Are these your signatures?"

Sure enough on Hernando's desk is a piece of paper with "Mary Blu" written over and over again. The snow storm in her head is letting up just a little bit as Mary begins puzzling over those signatures. "Roger, I don't think so. I know I didn't spend last night here writing my signature over and over again. I wonder…I wonder if maybe Hernando was practicing."

Roger looks at the sheet of paper then at Mary. His eyes bounce back and forth several times. Each glance seems to dampen his spirits a little more. "The picture is coming clear. I can now determine that Hernando forged your signature. Why didn't you tell me earlier?"

Mary doesn't know. Shaking her head she begins

describing the events of last night. "After I got home from work I talked with Hernando."

Roger's excitement rekindles. "You talked with Hernando?"

"Oh yes, I asked his permission to go into his desk so I could get those papers you needed."

"You told Hernando that I wanted papers from his desk?" Roger's face contorts in barely contained rage. "You told Hernando!"

At that very moment Rita makes her triumphal entrance into the office. "I goddamn knew it all the time!"

Mary attempts to organize herself into an apology. "I'm so sorry Rita."

Rita casts a withering glance at her partner before rushing to Roger, a lost girl now found. "Roger you saved me. You saved me, Roger!"

He smiles chivalrously.

From her champion's arms she returns her gaze to a baser character. "There's a new goddamn order around here! I'm in charge! I've watched this company go down the tubes because of you and Hernando. I'm the boss now!"

Roger smiles. "She," He looks at Mary with withering scorn, "warned Hernando."

Rita stares at Mary with an icy smile. "I knew it; they were in on it together." Her large hands squeeze into fists.

Roger nods, "I've called your lawyer Rita. She'll be

here in a few minutes. I think we should wait in my office. I'll be spending a lot of time here, a lot of time."

Mary stands so still that even her breath barely disturbs her chest. She stairs at Hernando's computer screen, his name written over and over again.

Chapter 47

Like some floating piece of debris Mary is drawn into the swirl of Roger's office. Within minutes a slim blond woman with an emerald ring enters the office as secretly as a whisper. Mary dimly realizes that she is the lawyer.

Roger starts the show. "I had it all figured out right from the start. When Rita came in and told me her story I knew there was foul play at large, a conspiracy of sorts." He stares at Mary.

That head of Mary's that seems barely anchored to her shoulders keeps nodding.

Roger's eyes pierce his dazed prey. "We know that Mary alerted Hernando last night so that he could make a safe get away."

The lawyer clicks her pen in a rhythm of anticipation...click, click, click.

The choreography climaxes. "Good damn fucker! Mary, you fucker!" Rita screams.

Roger supplies a temporary pause to the outrage by then giving a blow by blow description of his cunning. "Of course I am waiting for further developments. What do you think we ought to do about your friend, Mary?"

The lawyer lifts her attention from the emerald ring just long enough to nod to Roger and Rita.

Roger smiles innocently.

Mary hears that voice from the distance and musters one last resolve of determined care for the floundering company. "I think what Hernando did to Rita is terrible. But what I most care about is doing the best thing for the company. If that means to… that's what we need to do…I mean to pr..pr..prosecute Hernando."

Roger licks his lips, "And anyone else involved." He stares at Mary.

Rita jumps to her feet sputtering, "How dare you talk about the fucking good of this company! Your judgment is shit. Don't look so innocent, we're going to get you, to get you both and make you pay until you rot in hell." Her ham like fists thrashed the air as she fixes her wild eyes on Mary.

The lawyer resumes clicking her ball point pen. Roger keeps smiling; Mary sits motionless, eyes blank, nodding.

Fortunately for Mary, Rita has some very serious business to do somewhere and leaves. Mary forces herself back into the wheel of her urgent routines.

Sometime during that afternoon she receives a call. "Is this that stinker Mary?"

"Yes."

"My mommy says that we own the company now and that you, Mary, are a goner. Mommy knows all the ways you tried to cheat her. Bad Mary."

"I...I...I never intended to hurt her. I made a mistake. I'm so sorry. I...I...I."

"Mommy says being sorry isn't nearly enough, not for one minute. You stinker!" Click.

Chapter 48

And so starts Mary's final phase of her big business. She continues to report to work to keep The Rainbow going, but at home in the evening and weekends, she spends her time in front of an old black and white television on which Belinda had stored her paints. Except for a vertical roll that occasionally leaves Mary nauseated…well, it really doesn't matter anyway. That spring and summer she never misses *The Wheel of Fortune*. In fact other than dragging herself back and forth from work, *The Wheel of Fortune* is the center of her life. That half hour of television pulses out its significance throughout her entire day covering over her shame and confusion. For a half an hour every evening Mary is absorbed by watching the eager contestants call out different letters; then they spin the wheel of fortune which awards money or misfortune. If spared by the Wheel, contestants can guess the phrase that the letters spell out.

Two or three times a week Rita makes an appearance at The Rainbow and screams accusations at Mary. Mimi leaves Mary alone now. As for Roger, between reliving his moment of glory, firing the furnace of Rita's vengeance, and watching Mary closely; he has created a generous income source for himself. He intends to get ALL the conspirators even if he has to spend months. In fact he grows to enjoy the fine neighborhood of Fernwood and even joins The Fern Club.

It is a spring of ominous harmonies. In June once again the wheels within wheels of bureaucracy: the governor, legislature, and Department of Human Services under pressure from even larger forces in Congress which itself is reacting to some vague but frantic popular mandate, decides it is time to reorganize again, nothing dramatic of course except for the increased paperwork…all in the name of saving money. Someone somewhere decides that they don't want money spent on something as nebulous as mental illness. Services to mentally ill clients are to be cut back. Even before receiving the long and confusing letter from DHS, The Rainbow's clients can hear the screaming velocity accelerate as they spin further down into dread.

The roof of Mary's house springs another leak, this time in Belinda's room. Mortgage payments and fuel bills loom dangerously since Mary never opens mail now. She even forgets to notice spring; after all she needs to be ready for the Wheel of Fortune. She won't be caught off guard again.

One warm evening in June, windows shaded, the flicker of *The Wheel of Fortune* blaring on the television, Mary waits expectantly for that revelation of fortune. Unlike Mary's life this program is serenely controlled by the master of ceremonies. Mary sits in the darkened room, mouth open, waiting for the next message from on high. As the image on the television begins to roll a contestant begins jumping up and down. The excitement is contagious; Mary sits up straight and whispers, "He's got it! I think he's got it!" And sure enough as the contestant guesses, "TIME'S UP," bells ring, people cheer, the contestant jumps up and down in ecstasy.

Mary's eyes widen as the phrase flashes like a revelation across the screen. She sits motionless like Moses on Sinai, in dumb and blind awe. Some momentous secret that had been planted in a deep down dark spot within her is now emerging.

Late that night she wakes up, her pillow soaked as if it had been left out in the rain. She puts on her wrinkled nursing whites, walking firmly down the noisy stairs, and sits down in an old stuffed chair to wait for the sunrise. Round about 5 a.m. one bird call sets the whole fading black sky atwitter. The sun, like a large pink rosebud inches onto the horizon, and even while she watches, the sky turns blue. She perches on that moment like a very large bird on a wire.

Then she walks up to the bathroom to brush her

teeth with determination and skill. She looks at the image in the mirror, and perhaps because her gums are still tingling, for an instant, she knows that image is not her...not really anyway. There is something more, something deeper wakes inside herself. She rolls the deodorant on in broad courageous strokes, feeling the sliding smoothness on her arm pit. Then like a message revealing itself on *Wheel of Fortune*, she knows that she needs to sell that house of memories and her ragged share of The Rainbow...not frantic or hopeful choices; she just knows "TIME'S UP."

On her wild pathway to work she feels the ground pressing up underneath her and that special smell when summer warmth sets in for the day. The wild white achillea blooms and long spikes of mullein are knotted with swelling yellow flower buds. She hears gold finches, robins, and crows piercing through the lush summer green. And the sun, it feels like warm butter on her face.

Even before Rita can say, "This goddamn business isn't worth the pot I use to piss in and it's all your fault!" Mary says, "Rita, Time's up. I'm leaving."

Rita stands dazed, a lost look on her face as she begins wondering where that goddamn Mimi is.

Mary walks back to her desk but not to the hamster wheel of her anxiety and begins sorting papers. She wants to organize things as well as she can before leaving.

Rita leaves early on some urgent but ambiguous adventure.

Roger stops by Mary's desk; he looks disappointed as he says, "I couldn't find any paper trail for you, but it's still your fault."

Mary hears the wheel of fortune spinning.

As people come to The Rainbow this day with their problems and sorrows and hopes, she just stops what she is doing and listens. Sometimes all she can say is, "I don't know." At about 6:30 Mary unplugs the coffee pot and locks the door before she leaves.

Ariadne is cutting flowers in the front of Fern Hall. She notices Mary and gently motions for her to come over.

Mary walks up the sidewalk bordered in marigolds and stands in front of Ariadne.

They make eye contact. "Mary, why, hello. What a pleasure to see you. Come in and sit down." Ariadne takes the lead up those cracking limestone stairs and through the screen door.

Mary steps through into the cool. "I don't want to interrupt you or anything."

"This isn't anything; it's something."

Mary looks confused for a moment and then smiles. "I might want to talk with you for just a minute…if you have time, maybe."

"Sure, dear."

Mary lowers herself into a soft chair and feels the breeze filtering through the screen door. She can almost hear it. "Thanks for all the things you've done, letting your carriage house become The Rainbow, and your help at the Christmas party, but most of all for the times you've stopped to talk with me."

Ariadne nods graciously.

"There's been times in these last few months when everything seemed so confusing, like people thought about me in ways I didn't understand. I still don't really. I'm glad that you are here, sort of watching. I just want to tell you that last night I decided it's time to leave The Rainbow; funny how it isn't even a way to make everything all right."

Mary looks down for a moment, and then she straightens up in the chair. "Things aren't all right. It's funny how everything feels so torn away, leaving me sitting here." She pauses settling in to the situation. "Thanks for telling me all that stuff about your life."

For the longest moment Ariadne places a hand by her right ear as if she were listening carefully. "You know Mary, I don't hear it anymore."

"What's that?"

"That grating sound that I heard on the first visit that you three made here. The very first time in my life I really heard that sound was when my marriage to Ben was ending. That grating sound kept getting louder right up until one afternoon in the basement. After a spell of crying I remember staring at the drain and wondering what was different; something that I couldn't put my finger on had changed. And then I realized that, that grating sound had stopped, like a prayer answered. Since then I've thought about that sound especially since it periodically still pops up, usually when something very difficult is happening around me. I think difficulty is what that sound is all about. You see Mary to each of us, life is happening in no uncertain terms. Sometimes it's carefree like a May ride; other times it's like falling down a hole with no bottom, scaring the living be-Jesus out of you."

Ariadne sits in a moment of stillness. "I've figured that the scraping sound really comes from trying to dig in our heels. I think there is price to pay for that, a price to pay until you finally stop and feel the fall. At least that's what I did. That's when I realized that the grating sound is a signal for me to wiggle my toes, relax my hands and let go.

Mary's hands relax on her lap, her fingers softly move as if feeling for the first time.

Ariadne gently sways. "Things are like that sometimes."

Mary pauses, listening.

"There's no rush on things like this." Ariadne looks away for a moment, and then turns back to Mary. "I'm not one for dragging out goodbyes, so Mary Blu I'm just going to put these flowers in a vase." She stops, listening for something again. "On second thought, these are for you."

Chapter 49

During those next couple of weeks without a yellow brick road or the hope of a happy ending, Mary says goodbyes. When all her friends come through that door under The Rainbow, she asks them how they are, listens, and says goodbye. Sometimes she even smiles, although she lets that kind of sneak up on her. Of course periodically she sits down, rest her hands in her lap and wiggles her fingers and toes.

She finds a real estate agent who looks at her house, shakes his head, and says that he'll see what he can do. At work Mary finally has time to stop juggling all those urgent pieces of paper and organizes them in some recognizable order. Little accidents begin popping through holes in the net of her vigilance. One particularly hot day not even caring about the encroaching moisture under her arm pits, she takes a particularly generous gulp of water and feels that coolness drip down her chin under her blouse and slither in silvery delight between her breasts.

Rita is strangely quiet. At times she still looks at Mary with her fists clenched ready to continue bloody revenge, but then some vague unsettling perplexity seems to settle across her face and for the briefest of moments she appears to experience a confused and fleeting tenderness.

Rita has a last surprise. She loves parties. Since this is her company now, she can do whatever she wants, whenever she wants. She invites Roger who continues to spend his time looking into the books, and also Ariadne. Rita doesn't invite clients, after all Mary has betrayed their trust.

As the time really is up on Mary's final afternoon under The Rainbow, a little voice calls out, so very like Mimi's voice, from Roger's control center. "Mary, Mary quite contrary come into Roger's office. We've got a surprise for you."

Mary stands up from her tidy desk, falters just for a moment, and then responds to that invitation. As she enters the office she sees Rita's lustrous blueberry eyes peeking over a very, very large cake.

Rita is cozied up against Roger, like a child with her father. "It's a swell party isn't it Mary, even if you have been so naughty?"

Mary is listening now with a new alertness. She studies Rita as she snuggles up with Roger. She ponders the situation and quite unexpectedly asks, "To whom am I speaking?"

After a moment of shattered confusion, Rita's face hardens. "Get in here, this goddam party is supposed to be for you!"

Mary simple watches the transformation and begins wiggling her fingers subtly.

Ariadne enters to become the final celebrant. She has dressed that day in deep shades of purple, but braided into her gray hair is a scarf yellow and brilliant.

Rita is gleeful again. "Come on you guys let's start eating. Come on Mary say something. Do you like my cake Mary, do you?"

Mary's head bobs on her delicate neck for a moment, and then before Rita can resume, Mary rumbles her chair back and her whole body appears to be pulled up by the crown of her head. Before she knows it she is standing as high as the sun in June and speaking just as definitely. "It's so strange to be standing here on my last day of this big business. So much has happened."

Rita's hands lying next to the cake begin fisting.

Mary wiggles her toes and goes on. "I'm happy… not exactly happy…" She looks down in confusion for a moment and then straightens up, "Grateful sort of to be able to have done things I never dreamed of."

Again something like perplexity covers Rita's face.

"And that's all now, goodbye!" Mary sits down.

Ariadne nods in satisfaction and cuts a large slice of cake.

Rita jumps up and down eyes glittering, "Give it to me, to me, me!"

Ariadne hands the piece of cake to Mary, the guest of honor, and cuts a second piece for Rita.

At 5 pm under an avalanche of cake crumbs Rita announces the end of the party, after all she and Roger have very, very important tasks to do. They rush out of the room.

Mary stands up. "Well Ariadne, Time's up."

Ariadne rises. Her lipstick working its way up those cracks edging her lips, she approaches Mary.

Even before Mary can get embarrassed Ariadne begins undoing that gray and brilliant yellow braid, slowly like a silent dance in a room with no mirrors--a repeating elegance of unwinding. Her crispy hair now hangs loose, gray cascading to her waist. The brilliant scarf resting in her hands she speaks. "Now Mary, please bend down a minute."

Mary does.

Ariadne places both her hands behind Mary's thin neck and places that brilliant scarf around it. "Now Mary Blu, don't think that this is supposed to remind you of me. Granted if it does it's all right; but mostly it's to help you remember that you are not losing the rainbow today. This is just a business--a place. Your rainbow is something more mysterious spreading across the sky."

Scarf around her neck, Mary stands straight, tall and stately.

Ariadne looks up at her. "Now goodbye, Mary Blu."

Two weeks later a single man with three cats and a good job buys Mary's house.

Epilogue

After all the throwing out and cleaning there was very little Mary took with her to the rear apartment in the brown house standing in a neighborhood that was fast becoming downtown.

That first night as she lay in bed in her new residence emptied of happy endings she noticed the moon poking its head through those fluttery lace curtains that someone else had left behind like a forgotten grace. For the longest time she stared into that pale face staring back at her.

Perhaps the moon's overly long visit explained her irritability the next morning that dawned too soon. Even the sky hung so gray and stubborn that it refused to shine in her windows. The bed springs squeaked as she faltered onto the clammy floor. As she prepared breakfast, the tinny jangling of corn flakes tumbling was the only interruption in the sullen but mercifully quiet morning.

That's when she heard it, a banging, grating sound that shook tiny white parachutes out of a strangely familiar looking tree that framed her second story window.

Mary's face flashed like a distant summer storm before suddenly relaxing. She rested her hands in her lap and seemed to be doing something with her fingers--that intrusion continued to grind. That's when with a little more determination than absolutely necessary she stood up, shoved the chair back under the table, and sought the agent of that interruption.

She stepped out onto the top landing of a back stairway that perched in a dull steely sky filled with the throb of traffic sounds. Her gaze searched through the dusty leaves of that familiar tree towards an asphalt alley and a hard packed back yard.

Sure enough, a girl with not particularly clean hair in which a plastic pink barrette clung like a regret, was hitting a nearby trash can with punishing and automatic repetition.

"Hey you down there would you stop that!"

The girl kept at her occupation for a few more whacks before lifting up a thin face with eyes so dull they made the sky look blue. Then she took to whacking again.

Maybe it was those eyes, but Mary sat down, settling on that landing and listened to a familiar melody.

As if confused by the attention achieved, the girl

stopped of her own accord and glanced up. "Hey lady, what are you doing up there?"

Mary smiled. "Oh I'm just sitting here for a while."

"I bet this really bugs you lady, huh?" The little face looked up at Mary.

"First, my name is Mary. Second, I've heard more pleasant sounds, but that one isn't all that bad. What's your name?"

The girl's glance fluttered away and automatically her arms began threatening the garbage can.

Mary simply sat in that unpromising morning like a silent witness.

Perhaps not getting her accustomed response the girl looked bewildered and out of that unfamiliar opening came a voice. "My name's Rockie." She fastened a sideways glance onto Mary's face.

"Rockie, why that's a nice name. Is that the name you were born with?"

The girl dropped the stick. Maybe it got in the way of her more confidential tone. "It's really Roxanne, but that's hard to say, and besides I hate it. It's almost as bad as my last name."

Mary nodded in deep sympathy. "I suppose that some names can almost do you in. Can I be so bold as to ask you what your last name is?"

"Aw, it's a stupid name. You promise you won't make fun of me?"

"Ya Rockie, I promise, cross my heart."

"Crabtree, Crabtree, Crabtree, that's what it is.

All the kids at school say "crabby, crabby, nobody likes a crabby."

Quite rightly Mary took some time to let this settle in, no longer given to quick reassurances. Finally rubbing her chin she answered. "Why Rockie, have you ever seen a crab tree?"

The question just hung there free of any demand. Rockie looked at Mary with something just short of curiosity.

Mary settled her large form more comfortably onto that landing. "Well, crab trees are really beautiful, in fact they're one of my personal favorites. In spring they're covered with blossoms so pink that they outshine that pretty pink barrette in your hair. And that's not all. At the end of summer they are covered with little bright red apples that have a tingly aftertaste that tickles your mouth with delight. They make the best jelly in the whole world. Not like that pale store bought apple jelly. I guess that's all right if you like things that don't have much character, but crab apple jelly is so red that when the sun passes through it looks like a sparkling red jewel. And the taste, the taste is spectacular. It's sweet, but there's a wildness that just begs you to keep spreading it on bread and placing it in your mouth. Granted, it's not for people with ordinary tastes."

Those tight little eyes started measuring out a smile that almost by accident spilled out and spread out over her face. "Is that really true lady--Mary?"

"Sure Rockie." She sat ponderous like a mountain.

"You gonna be here for the rest of the summer, Mary?"

"I'll be around my dear."

"You can call me Roxanne, Roxanne Crabtree. You sure you're gonna be around?"

"I sure hope so, Roxanne Crabtree." Mary paused for a moment as if remembering something which she had forgotten. "By the way, next time you can just holler up. You don't need to bang that stick."

The End

Exxtras: After some strategic ads potential employees also begin showing up under that arc too, many of them long ago washed up on the shores of their own dread--eccentric people, who don't bat an eye at the strange trio at the heart of this enterprise.